Herbert Best and his puli

Desmond and Dog Friday

HERBERT BEST

Desmond and Dog Friday

Illustrated by W. T. Mars

The Viking Press   New York

For Margaret Morrow,
addict of the Desmond tales,
and warmly approved by our
own foundling dog Friday

chapter one

Gus and Desmond splashed their way happily out to Treasure Island. It was one of those warm summer mornings that would turn hot later on, and nothing very much was liable to happen. But the wet felt pleasant to hot paws, and Gus had tied his sneakers by their strings around his neck so they wouldn't get soaked.

The Island was small and tidy: small enough so you would range all over it on a lazy morning and small enough to be owned by the boys and girls of Newtown. From Gus's side of the town a short walk across a field led down to the riverbank facing the Island. Here the water ran brown and shallow over the stones and in midsummer Gus could skip across on the stones and Desmond could cross almost dry-pawed, or he could slip in and swim in the cool water that went *lap lap lap* and felt so good on a hot day. On the other side of the Island the water was deeper, and the big boys used it for a swimming hole.

It was said that two warring tribes, the Land Indians and the Canoe Indians, had called the big smooth rock in the center of the Island their Council Rock, and there were signs of long vanished campfires. Three tall pines shaded the rock and turned the Island into a pirate craft, whenever you wanted one, or in a twinkling of an eye the pines could become coconut palms, and there you were, on Robinson Crusoe's island, or Treasure Island. And if you had been learning about Columbus at school your ship could land on one of the two small beaches to discover the New World. It was a grand place to come on a hot day, with sandwiches in your pocket and a bone for your dog. Newtown was proud of its little Island.

Gus's present adventure was to get out to the beach without touching a rock, or anyway not a dry rock. Gus's legs were short, and Desmond's were even shorter. He had to swim for part of the way with his white-tipped tail stretching out behind like a rudder.

Desmond was the first to splash ashore because he was scout for the Landing Party. He shook the water out of his coat and began right away to look along the beach for clues. Gus came up close behind. Desmond was the first to discover the footprint. He smelled it. Then Gus saw it too.

8

"Oh," said Gus. "Friday! Just like in *Robinson Crusoe*."

Desmond had thought today was Wednesday, but in summertime with no school you lost count of the days.

The footprint hadn't been made by a man, but by a dog, a small dog. It wasn't Alf's footprint, because Alf didn't much like water. It wasn't Gloria's. She was a sheep dog, and anyway, almost never left her little ones long enough to come out to the Island. And certainly the print was too small for Bill the boxer, even if Bill ever traveled far from his own doghouse. In fact Desmond didn't think that the pawmark belonged to any of the Newtown dogs.

Puzzling, thought Desmond.

"Puzzling," said Gus, who was always quick to get what Desmond was thinking.

More pawmarks ran inland. "We'll have to follow them and find out who they belong to," said Gus. He dropped his voice to a whisper because maybe the marks might belong to somebody dangerous—like cannibals.

So they went along very quietly, up under the pine trees toward the center of the Island, which wasn't far. They lost the trail in a patch of weeds, but Desmond cast about and sniffed. He had a good nose. You have to have a good nose for clues if you are a Private Eye, or even the scout for an Expedition. They found the trail again, then lost it beside the flat rock.

"It rained last night," said Gus. "Let's go look in the cave."

That was just what Desmond had planned to do. Gus was still talking in whispers, so Desmond didn't bark.

The cave was a small one, only big enough to crawl into if you crouched down. Then Desmond couldn't help barking because there was somebody in the cave. Out crawled Dog Friday!

She was small and not much to look at. Her gray coat was tangled with burrs, and her ears and tail drooped because she was sad and even frightened. Gus held out a cautious hand for her to sniff. It smelled of jam and peanut butter from the sandwiches in his pocket.

"Poor Friday," said Gus, reassuring the little pooch. "You were out in last night's storm, were you? And you look as though you'd been hungry for days."

It was early to have lunch but Desmond sniffed at Gus's pocket, to remind him. Gus hauled out the bag of sandwiches, which were squashed and rather damp. You didn't go exploring without taking rations along, even a bone. The bone, not a big one, was in Gus's other pocket.

Desmond was glad to note that Friday had good manners. Though she must be very hungry she didn't snap at the food. Gus and Desmond ate only a little, so there would be more for her.

"Where do you come from?" Gus asked her.

Friday wriggled apologetically. Of course she couldn't tell. Even Desmond, smart as he was, didn't know the names of the Newtown streets, though he knew the house of every dog with a boy.

Desmond hinted at the other pocket, and Gus pulled out the bone. Friday took it gently in her teeth and with a glance at Desmond trotted away to hide it. The Island had always

been a great place for bones, since after a picnic every dog
hid his bone there in case there mightn't be one for him on the
next trip.

"We can't just leave her here," said Gus.

That was what Desmond was about to think. They sat down
to consider it.

"We'll take her home and get Mother to phone around to
ask who's lost a dog"—which was a little puzzling because

it wasn't a dog that was lost. She was right here. It was her owners who were missing.

So all three of them splashed back across the river, and when Friday had shaken the mud and water out of her coat she looked a lot better; the kind of dog that would have nice owners.

Gus's mother was busy in the kitchen, and lovely cooking smells drifted out. She saw them coming and called through the window, "Isn't that a strange dog, Gus? Where did you find it?"

Gus came up on the back porch. "We found her on the Island," he explained. "We don't know where she belongs."

Mother said, "Look at her dog tag."

Desmond wondered why he hadn't thought of that himself. But when Gus looked under Friday's long, thick coat he saw that she didn't have a tag. She didn't even have a collar. No wonder she was lost. Desmond had a red-leather collar with gold-looking studs in it, and a dog tag, besides his Private Eye badge—the one that Gus had got out of a box of cereal.

Mother agreed to telephone around and ask about a lost dog. "Though without a dog tag I hardly know where to start," she said.

"You know what?" Gus told Desmond. "You'll have to do some more detecting, you lazy old dog you. We'll go on down to Mr. Mason's drugstore and begin there. Most every boy and dog in Newtown goes there some time or other. Somebody's bound to recognize her."

Desmond knew that it wasn't going to be as simple as that. If Dog Friday belonged in Newtown, even right over beyond the railroad tracks, she would have known where she lived and found her way back home. And if she didn't know, how could anyone else?

The drugstore was very convenient, just down the street a bit. Gus led the way, Desmond and Friday trotting behind. But when Gus opened the screen door Desmond slipped in first, just in case someone had left an ice-cream cone lying around. He licked his nose to dampen it, and snuffled twice, as a good detective should. The nice smells and scents were just the same as last time they had been here. There were scents of soap and perfumes from bottles and boxes that people bought when they wanted to take a bath or to look pretty. But nearer the counter there were better smells, like coffee and frying bacon and eggs and hamburgers.

The drugstore cat, whose name was Seven-up, though nobody knew why, jumped down from the counter to rub against Gus's leg. She knew both Gus and Desmond. When she was the drugstore kitten Desmond and Gus—well anyway Gus— had rescued her from a high tree.

Gus said, "Hello, Seven-up," and slid onto a stool beside the counter where there were doughnuts and cakes and other nice things under plastic domes. He said, "Good morning, Mr. Mason," to Mr. Mason, who was wearing a clean white coat, so as not to get his suit dirty.

Mr. Mason picked up the ice-cream scoop. "Not seen you around for a day or two, Gus. The same?" and he held the scoop ready to dip.

Gus shook his head. He already owed Mr. Mason fifteen cents and didn't want to run up too big a bill. Desmond gave a gulp. His mouth had been getting ready for the tip end of the ice-cream cone that Gus always saved for him.

"Who's your new friend?" asked Mr. Mason, wiping a glass and nodding toward Friday.

Gus said he didn't know, and explained how he and Desmond had found Dog Friday on the Island.

"She looks as though she could do with some food," said Mr. Mason. And he set down a dish of half-melted chocolate and strawberry ice cream that somebody had left unfinished on the counter. Why anyone would go off without finishing their ice cream was hard to guess, but maybe they didn't own a dog to help them tidy up.

Friday sniffed at the dish, gave it a little lick, as though this was something she had never tasted before, then gobbled it right down and waved her tail at Mr. Mason to say "Thank you." She had a nice tail, thick and plumey, though it didn't have a handsome white tip like Desmond's.

The door opened and in came a tall man in uniform. It was the state trooper. He said, "Hi, Gus!" and scratched Desmond's head in passing. They were old friends, because the trooper had worked on several of Desmond's cases. Maybe he could use him on this one.

The trooper looked at Friday and asked, "Desmond taken on an assistant? There are times when I could use one myself."

Gus explained all over again.

"I see," said the trooper. "So you're trying to find who she belongs to. Best thing is to advertise, but that costs money. Quite a lot of money."

"Not here, it doesn't," said Mr. Mason, wiping another

glass. "Most everybody in town comes in here. We'll write out a notice and put it on that board by the door." He pushed a pencil and paper across the counter to Gus. "You write it out, Gus, and I'll pin it up by the phone."

Desmond sat down and scratched his ear. Writing out a notice was something he hadn't done before. Neither had Gus. Desmond thought hard. Gus sucked his pencil and thought too.

Gus printed out *LOST* in big letters at the top of the page.

"That's right," said Mr. Mason, leaning over the counter to watch. "Now you say what's lost, so people will know it's a wallet, or whatever."

That made it easy. So Gus printed, *OWNERS OF DOG FRIDAY ON ISLAND.* Saying where she had been lost was Gus's own idea. Desmond grinned approval.

"Now you want to give a description," said the trooper, sipping his Coke.

But how could you describe the owners if you didn't know what they looked like?

"I've never seen them," said Gus.

"Oh," said the trooper. "Then the best you can do is to say what the dog looks like." And they all turned to look at her, even Seven-up the cat.

"Skye terrier, maybe?" said Mr. Mason.

"Not all Skye terrier," said the trooper. "Coat too long, tail too fluffy. Here, let's see how old you are." Friday good-naturedly let him open her mouth to look at her teeth, though she sneezed because he tickled her whiskers. "Not more than two years old I'd say. Maybe a year and a half."

It was quite a nice notice when Gus had finished printing it. Mr. Mason pinned it up right away as he had promised and said he would phone Gus if anyone asked about a lost dog. Gus asked the trooper to keep an eye out for anybody who looked as though their dog had lost *them,* which seemed more sensible to Desmond.

"Sure, I'll do just that," said the trooper as he paid for his Coke.

Maybe it was because of the notice going up, or maybe it was because of the ice cream, but Friday was looking a little better all the time. As they were walking back home she put her nose into Gus's hand to say "Thank you."

All the same there was going to be a lot of detecting for Desmond to do. How did you find people when you hadn't any idea who you were looking for, what they looked like, or what they smelled like?

This was certainly the toughest case he and Gus had ever handled, even though they had the trooper to help them.

chapter two

They sat on the front lawn, Desmond and Gus and Friday. They were doing nothing special, because there was nothing special to do on a hot morning in July. Gus leaned back against the trunk of the big elm, chewed a piece of grass, and wriggled his bare toes. Friday was pulling a burr out of her long coat and Desmond sniffed at the warm breeze. A good nose often told you something was about to happen before your eyes or ears could catch it.

This time it was a loud *buzz-buzz-buzz* that made him prick up his ears. The sound didn't come from one of the cars on the street beyond the fence, nor from a truck or motorcycle, because there weren't any in sight. It stopped at the gate.

"Someone's given Chubby a roarer for his bike," said Gus. "I wonder what he'll have next."

And sure enough it was Chubby. He leaned his bicycle against the porch and came across the lawn. Desmond went to meet him with a friendly tail-wave, but Friday stayed put. She didn't seem very partial to boys, the way most dogs were.

"It can't be Desmond," said Chubby as he squatted down beside Gus. "It must be that new dog." And he looked at Friday.

"What must be?" said Gus, who had stopped chewing his grass stalk.

"The dog in the Newtown *Gazette*. My dad said someone was advertising a dog, and gave the telephone number. I knew it was yours so I came around. My dad thinks I ought to own a dog."

Chubby owned just about everything else, from swimfins to roller skates, though nobody ever saw him using them. That was maybe why he was so plump and people called him Chubby, though his real name was Charles. If anyone ever needed a dog to show him how to live and have adventures it was this Chubby.

Gus was puzzled. You could tell by the way he frowned. Chubby put out a plump, cautious hand to stroke Friday, the way you would stroke a cat, not pat a dog. Any dog that took on Chubby would have to start teaching him right from the very beginning.

"Only I don't much want a dog," Chubby went on. "I'd have to spend too much time looking after him, and I wouldn't know how."

Desmond had to bite back a grin. Boys didn't look after dogs, except to open doors and things like that. Dogs looked after boys. Newtown dogs did anyway.

"You know how people get numbers wrong over the phone," Gus said slowly. "Maybe the ad was phoned in to the *Gazette*. I wouldn't even let you borrow Desmond because I need him. And Friday isn't ours to give away until Father buys her a license and a dog tag. And he can't yet, because we're still looking for her owners."

"Gee, Gus, that's great!" Chubby scrambled to his feet. "I'll tell Dad just how it is as soon as he gets home. And if you want to borrow my bike, or the swimfins or the tennis racket or anything, you're welcome to them."

And Chubby was out through the gate and getting onto his bicycle before Gus could even say, "Thanks a lot."

Gus shoved into his sneakers and stood up. "You know what Desmond? There's kind of a mystery here. I don't know anyone in town who'd want to give away his own dog. I'll go ask Mother about it."

A mystery? Yes, that was what Desmond had thought it was too. And naturally Gus would need Desmond to start solving it. So he and Friday got up and followed Gus. A lovely smell of roasting meat floated out through the screen door. He had to lick his lips and swallow.

"No, don't come in, Desmond," said Gus from the kitchen. "You know what Mother thinks about dogs that stand around and lick their lips and look half starved. Stay outside now." And the screen door closed almost on Desmond's nose.

Desmond looked at Friday. Friday looked at Desmond, but

she didn't say anything. She never did. Desmond said, "Chubby's all right, only nobody has ever trained him. It's too late to start now. Why don't we go look for a boy that's properly dog-trained already? There's lots of them around here. Bill the boxer has two boys, and they do almost everything he wants. But he never exercises them properly, so maybe he would like you to help."

Friday wagged her plumey tail in agreement.

As they trotted up Main Street Desmond wanted to tell Gus, for he saw what a bright idea this was going to be. If Friday found her own people she might go away and he would never see her again. But if she settled in Newtown he could see her whenever he wanted to. Then, too, she would have a home of her own and nobody would say, "Now Desmond, guests come first!" or "That's Friday's drinking bowl, not yours, Desmond!" And anyway, that would be Bill's problem.

Bill was in his doghouse. In the past he had won more ribbons than you could begin to count on all four paws, but lately he had retired so that he could spend more of his valuable time thinking. His two boys had built him a fine doghouse to do his thinking in, and there he was this morning, lying in the shade. His eyes were closed, to show how deep in thought he was.

He opened one eye, for politeness's sake. "What's your problem today, Desmond?" he growled in his deep voice. "Detecting again? If so, you've come to the right person for advice."

20

Desmond told him about finding Friday on the Island. Friday said nothing, as usual. Bill opened the other eye to look at her.

"I've seen a dog like her at a dog show once. Maybe the name of the breed will come back to me. I don't recall it now." He thought a moment longer. "She probably didn't go out to the Island alone, or she would have known where to walk back to. She must have got there in some other way." He sighed deeply and thought some more. You could always see Bill the boxer *thinking*. "In my young days when I used to have time to go to the Island on the boy's picnics we often swam on the other side of the place, and sometimes we even took our boat."

Of course! By boat! That was how Friday got there! That

was why she had left no trail to follow home. Desmond would have thought of that himself if he hadn't been so rusty with his detecting. But Friday should have told him that. All that she seemed able to say was "Yes" and "No," and even that didn't sound like Newtown English.

Bill caught the idea. He said, "Likely she is of some foreign breed and hasn't learned much of our language. You'll have to learn what language she does speak, Desmond. It would be good for you and would broaden your horizon."

Oh, no! Oh, no! Boys and girls learned foreign languages in school. Gus had explained that to him, though it seemed rather silly. Better to spend the time in learning to bark a dog language properly. There was a better idea. It came to Desmond like a flash, but he thought awhile how to put it to Bill; sweeten it up, so Bill would swallow it whole.

"Look, Bill, why don't you invite Friday to stay here with you and learn English? She couldn't find a better teacher. Meanwhile you could learn her language too. There isn't another dog in all Newtown with your brains and ability to teach."

"No time for that," growled Bill in his deep voice. "Besides I won't share my boys with anyone." He put it bluntly. "It takes both of them to look after me properly." He got up, stalked into his doghouse, and turned his back to lie down. The interview was finished.

Desmond and Friday trotted off. They ran into Gloria the German sheep dog taking her three little girls for their usual walk. When Desmond stopped to talk with her and explain about Friday being lost, she was sympathetic, and said how sad it must be to lose your humans. But after all it must have been Friday's own fault, for being careless with them.

Desmond suggested that Gloria might like Friday to come along and help look after the children.

Gloria looked very stern. "If your little friend can't keep an eye on her own grownups, she's not to be trusted with little ones. Do have a little sense, Desmond." And glancing right and left for an approaching car, she herded her small charges across the road.

Their next encounter was with Alf the airedale, which was not surprising. Wherever you went you were liable to run into Alf. His family were away a lot and he was supposed to live with a neighbor. But as he had no boy to look after, he spent most of his time getting into some kind of trouble. And he enjoyed every minute of it.

"Wanna wrestle, Des old man?" he asked as he so often did. He was so good-natured and so loved a fight that he would start one with almost anybody. When Desmond explained that they were just out for a walk, Alf asked, "How's the little pooch? Mind if I join you?"

Desmond explained that he was out to try to find a boy for Friday to look after, and was very busy. Alf didn't take the hint. He said he would come along too, because you never knew when you would run into a nice fight. He wasn't a thinking dog. He did things first and maybe thought about them later, if at all. He was certainly not the kind of assistant you wanted along when you were on a difficult piece of detective work. And it was because of Alf that the trouble started.

Popsey the poodle was on her front lawn, teaching Ellen, her girl, to hold up a hoop so she could practice her high jumps. Desmond pushed open the low swing gate and led the way in.

Ellen said, "Hello, Desmond. Come to call?" Then she caught sight of Alf and yelled, "Go away, you horrid dog! You've chewed the corner off the newspaper two mornings and upset the garbage pail twice." And she threw the hoop at him.

Desmond, Friday, and Alf didn't wait to open the gate again. They jumped it. You don't stop to argue with a girl.

It began to look as though the same thing was going to happen most everywhere. At one house Alf got into an argument, all very friendly, with a large tomcat. The cat won. At other places the dogs were away, or they declined to share their boy or girl. The only strange thing about the morning's walk was that as they went down the street almost every woman and even a couple of the men stopped to pat Friday and to talk to her. These were the same people who saw Alf and Desmond week after week and never even noticed them.

Each time Friday stood up on her furry bearlike hind legs, put two furry mitten paws on the strangers knees, and peered through her thick bangs at the stranger's face it looked as though she were greeting an old friend. She even licked a face or two. One woman exclaimed, "Oh, you little darling!" and kissed Friday in return.

Alf glanced sideways at Desmond. Desmond glanced back at him, not knowing what to say. If either of them had tried that trick, he would have been told, "Keep your dirty paws to yourself, you great clumsy brute!" How did Friday get away with it?

Desmond was thinking hard. He was putting two and two together as a good detective should. He knew now that Friday was probably a foreigner, and that her people had come from up- or down-river. Now he guessed that her owners were grownups, not boys and girls.

He had started to add this all up when a voice called: "Desmond! Desmond!"

It was Gus of course.

A car drew up right ahead and Gus jumped out and came running back. Right there, in front of Alf, Gus stooped and hugged Desmond as though he had been lost for days.

Alf was grinning from ear to ear and you couldn't blame him. Desmond could only be thankful that Gus hadn't disgraced them both by kissing him. Friday and Desmond followed Gus back to the car and hopped in. It was the reporter's car, and the reporter, an old friend, said, "Hi, Desmond! Who's your little pal?"

When Gus introduced Friday, the reporter said, "So this is the dog your father advertised in the Newtown *Gazette?* The ad said 'crossbreed' but this ain't any mutt. She's got class, this little lady. I've got to take her picture."

Gus thought to himself, so that's why Chubby came around asking about a dog that I was supposed to be giving away.

The reporter picked up his camera, jumped out, and took a picture of Friday sitting on the back seat, looking as though she owned the whole car.

Desmond waved his plumey tail, hoping the reporter would

snap a picture of him too, maybe with his Private Eye tag showing. He had once had his picture in the paper just that way. But the man climbed back into the car.

"Home now, I guess?" He made a U turn and started back along Main Street.

Desmond was thinking that he ought to have stopped and knocked that silly grin off Alf's face, but he pricked up his ears when Gus said, "If you put Friday's picture in the Newtown *Gazette* maybe her people will see it, and come for her."

"There's too many lost dogs for one of them to make a real story," said the reporter. "Hey! But wait a moment! Didn't you say you found her on the Island? The Island is getting to be news right now. The county wants to cut a new road and throw a bridge across the river, using the Island to support one of its piers. That would cut out Route 123 and save a few miles between towns. Newtown is dead set against it of course. It's the out-of-towners that want it."

Desmond pricked up his ears again. Gus couldn't, but he asked, "You mean they're going to take *our* Island to hold up a bridge across the river? Even though it doesn't belong to them?"

"That's about the shape of it, Gus. Unless we can get all Newtown out to vote against it," the reporter admitted. "Maybe my editor will let me run Friday's photo and a story about 'Dog Lost on Our Island.' Anything about the Island should be hot news right now."

Of course it was Desmond who should have his picture in

the paper. All Friday had done was to get lost. Desmond had found her.

It wasn't long before he had something even more exciting to think about. For as soon as the reporter had put them down near home, Gus whispered, "You know what, you old dog you?"

Desmond didn't, so Gus had to explain. "We can't let those out-of-towners steal our Island. We've got to save it. Somehow."

He couldn't say any more, because when they got to the porch they heard the telephone ringing and ringing, with nobody at home to answer it. So they all rushed in and Gus picked up the receiver and said "Yes?" and listened, and said "Yes," again, once or twice.

He put his hand over the phone and told Desmond, "It's a man who says he lost his dog on the Island. Only I don't think he did."

Then Gus asked the phone, "When would that be, mister?" and put his hand over the phone again to tell Desmond, "He says 'three days ago.' "

Desmond could see that the man-on-the-phone was mistaken. Three days ago wouldn't have given poor Friday enough time to become so scared and hungry and full of burrs. He gave a small whine to warn Gus to be very careful what he said. The man wasn't to be trusted, especially over the telephone, which takes away a person's smell.

Gus was still listening to the phone, and looking from Desmond to Friday and back again to Desmond. He must have heard that warning whine, for he said, "That dog you lost, mister, he wouldn't be a kind of a biggish dog, with a shiny black coat, a white-shirt front and a plumey tail with a white tip?"

For a moment Desmond didn't know what to think. It was Desmond himself that Gus was describing! But then he realized what a smart little guy his boy was, and Gus put his hand over the phone and whispered, "The man says yes, that's his dog all right, and to tell him this address and he'll be right over to pick him up."

Gus made his voice as deep as he could, and told the man, "Well mister, your dog's the spittin' image of our dog and I've got five dog tags to prove he's been ours ever since he was a pup. Good-by!" And he put the receiver back.

Desmond thumped his tail on the floor to show Gus how pleased he was that he had taken his warning, and how clever Gus had been to think of so neat a trick. But Gus still looked worried. He said to Friday, "That man's never seen you. He wanted to *steal* you. Like the reporter says that the 'bridge people' want to steal our Island. We'll have to be mighty smart, all three of us, and think up a plan to stop them."

Desmond thumped his tail on the floor again. Gus was right. He and Gus would think up a plan somehow.

chapter three

Desmond was feeling great as he trotted back home. He had chased that fat woodchuck out of the garden and into its hole in the meadow. Gus had whistled Friday into the house, which was just as well since a granddaddy woodchuck has long sharp teeth.

The front screen door was not quite closed. When Gus was being extra specially careful not to let it slam behind him, the spring didn't catch it shut. Desmond scratched the opening a little wider with his right front paw, so he could get his nose in. Now came the trick. His nose held the door so he could get his paw around the edge and give it a pull. Now it swung wide open, and he could scrabble in before the door swung back and caught his tail.

Any dog could push open a screen door from the inside, but only Desmond could sometimes open it from the outside. He wished little Friday had been there to see him do it. But Gus was in the kitchen now, so that was where she would be too. Gus had scarcely let her out of his sight since that man on the phone had tried to steal her.

Desmond was being extra cautious too. That was why, instead of running straight back to the kitchen to let Gus know he had scared off the woodchuck, he stopped in the hallway to sniff. He caught a whiff of someone who didn't belong there.

He knew it was a woman, but it was hard to tell one woman from another by her scent, because she bought it in a bottle. When a woman bought a new kind of perfume, or two of them used the same kind, it was very confusing to a detective.

But this woman didn't seem to use perfume, and she hadn't carried the faintest trace of dog or cat or tobacco or cooking, or anything nice. Desmond trotted into the living room where the scent was a little stronger, though it was mixed with the aroma of coffee. Now he had it! It was the scent of a newly-ironed cotton dress, but with it was the trace of the warning odor that humans give off when they are angry. All dogs learn it, so they can keep away from trouble.

Desmond was more than just a dog. He was a Dog Detective. He sat down near the chair where the scent was clearest, and scratched behind his right ear to make thinking easier. And right away he got the clue. The coffee!

30

There was nothing on the little table near the chair. Not a cup, not a crumb of cake. He got up and looked to make sure. But the coffee aroma indicated that the woman had been drinking coffee here. If she had been one of Mother's real friends she would have been asked into the kitchen. That wasn't much of a deduction, but it made Desmond feel better, because there were too many women in Newtown for him to recognize them all by their scent.

He trotted along to the kitchen just in time to hear Mother explaining to Gus about the visitor.

"She came to tell me to be sure that your father and I attend the meeting, and that we vote in favor of the new road and bridge," said Mother. "You know what Mrs. Nelson's like. She doesn't ask you; she practically orders you!"

Mrs. Nelson? Desmond's ears pricked up. She lived several blocks away and dogs kept clear of her. She wanted to have laws passed to have all dogs tied up at home, or taken to walk on a leash. No wonder he hadn't recognized her scent!

Mother wiped the second coffee cup and put it back on the shelf. "Well, I wouldn't promise, and she wouldn't leave. So I changed the subject and talked about our little orphan Friday. At first she said that all stray dogs should be sent to the dog pound. Then I told her what a nice, well-behaved dog little Friday was, and how badly she needed a good home and a nice mistress. Mrs. Nelson said, 'Send her around to me.' "

Oh, no! thought Desmond.

"Oh, no!" said Gus.

But there it was. Mother had almost promised. Now she glanced at Friday. "Better take her around right away and get it over with. But give her a good brushing first so she'll look as nice as possible."

Gus nodded glumly, and reached up on the shelf for the brush. Desmond followed Gus and Friday outside and they all sat down on the lawn. Gus picked up the brush and Desmond pushed forward for the usual grooming, which he loved, because it made his coat shine so. But Gus gave him only a few strokes of the brush, and didn't even touch his beautiful white-shirt front. He said, "That'll have to do for you now, Desmond," and set to work on Friday.

He brushed and brushed and even used the comb. Desmond had to stand there and watch and wait. He was fond of Friday, and sorry for her because she had lost her people. He had let her drink from his drinking bowl, and had been careful not to gobble up her food after he had finished his own. But no dog likes to share his boy, and Desmond wasn't even getting a fair share of the grooming. If anyone else had asked to adopt Friday he would have been pleased. But not Mrs. Nelson. He gave a sigh.

Gus heard it. "We won't be losing Friday altogether, Desmond," he said. "You can go over and take her for a walk whenever you want." He tried to sound cheerful, but he didn't look it. "Or Friday can come here for a visit if Mrs. Nelson will let her. I don't think she will though, because she doesn't like dogs wandering around loose, or cats either. But maybe," he added doubtfully, "it would be all right if we both went and fetched her sometimes."

Mother called Gus into the house to sponge off his knees, which were green from kneeling on the grass, and to put on a clean pair of sneakers. She said how nice Friday looked, but didn't even glance at Desmond.

Friday, who didn't yet know Mrs. Nelson, trotted along happily, tail up and nose in the air. They weren't far down the street when Gus said, "I don't think Friday's going to be happy there." He might have got that thought from Desmond. Oh, dear, it would have been so much better if they had been able to find her real owner!

Gus said, "Let's stop at Mr. Mason's first. We'll ask if people have been reading the notice we put up."

Midmorning the drugstore was almost always empty. There was a truck driver at the counter eating eggs and bacon, maybe for his lunch or maybe for his breakfast. Mr. Mason, in his white coat behind the counter, said, "Hi Gus! Hi Desmond!" and then remembered to say, "Hi, Friday!" And Seven-up jumped down from the end of the counter to touch noses with Desmond.

There was Gus's notice all right, tacked up beside the telephone booth. But nobody had left any message.

"One way or another," remarked Mr. Mason, "there must have been thirty or more people who have read it. And talked about it too. Now if only we had a photo of the little lost dog it might help."

Gus agreed. Then he looked in his pocket. There were only three pennies there and a tangle of string, and of course his knife. Desmond knew what he was looking for: the price of an ice-cream cone. Friday had run up to the man who was eating his lunch–breakfast and stood up on her hind paws and held up her forepaws the way she did to so many people she met. She always made a hit with the grownups, and that was what happened now.

The man patted her head and said, "You've got lots of class, little lady." Just what the reporter had said! "She hasn't found an owner yet? I'd take her myself, only my landlady doesn't like dogs." Then he added, "Does the little pooch like ice cream? How about a vanilla cone for her, George? Better make it three, while you're about it, one each for the pooch's two friends." He pulled some coins out of his pocket.

So this time it was really Friday who treated them all. Desmond preferred chocolate to vanilla, and Mr. Mason knew that. But it wasn't good manners to· say what you wanted when it was somebody else's treat.

As Gus got down from the high stool, Mr. Mason said, "It's too soon to give up hope, Gus. Your friend the trooper is keeping a sharp eye out for anyone who looks as though he had owned a dog like Friday. He's told the other men at the barracks too."

They all went out, feeling a lot more cheerful, though maybe it was only the pleasant feel of a whole ice-cream cone in their stomachs, and the last taste of it on their tongues.

Mrs. Nelson's house was quite a big one, for only one woman, and it didn't even look as though anyone lived there at all. It was all so clean and tidy, with no swing on the front porch, nor even a chair. The garden bed on the lawn inside the low picket fence was planted all in exact circles and squares, without a single weed in sight. Even the plants were staked up and tied, the way she wanted dogs to be.

Gus had just put his hand on the latch of the gate when Alf bounced up. "You're looking down at the tail, all three of you," he said. "How's about a wrestle, Des, old man, to cheer you up?"

Desmond didn't really want to be cheered up. At the sight of Mrs. Nelson's house he had begun to feel fine and gloomy again. Then he bristled all down his back. He had just recalled how Alf had laughed when Gus had jumped out of the reporter's car and hugged him.

"Attaboy!" barked Alf, seeing the bristles. "Good old Des!" and made a rush at him.

Well, you know how a friendly dog fight goes, with barking and snapping and grabbing each other and all the noise in the world. One grabs another by the leg, and throws him down. And then right away the other dog's on top, and barking and snarling at the top of his lungs. The more noise the better the fight. Most humans think that the dogs are tearing each other to pieces but they're really having as grand a time as boys playing football.

Gus shouted, "No, Desmond! No!" but not as though he really meant it.

Friday seemed to think that this was a real battle, and tried to stop it. Or maybe she was trying to help her friend, Desmond. She got in between Alf and Desmond, and was rolled over in the gutter. She scrambled up again, quick as a cat. She batted at Alf with her front paws, the way a cat might do. Maybe she had never tried to fight before and didn't know how. All she did was to get in the way. But there was good dog courage hidden under all that long fur, and though she got rolled in the gutter again and again, she still came back to help.

Alf jumped the low fence, so as to be clear of her. Desmond followed. Friday leaped after them. They all landed in a big square flower bed, which was lovely and soft to chase one another around in. Gus had just waded into the bed to shoo them all back to the road—fighting in other people's garden beds simply wasn't allowed—when the front door opened.

Out came a short, plumpish woman in a clean white apron. Mrs. Nelson. She was carrying an umbrella that she must have picked up from the stand just inside the door. She brandished it at them and began to open and close it the way Desmond had seen a scared woman do to a cow in a pasture.

"Get off my flower beds! Oh, my flower beds!" she shouted at them.

She waved the umbrella toward Alf, but he was used to dodging anything from brooms to golf clubs. He jumped over the fence and stood grinning at them through the gate.

Desmond would have followed him, but he had to stay and protect his boy. He stood right in front of Gus and growled a little. Mrs. Nelson flapped open her umbrella again, to scare him away. He stood his ground and was wondering if it would be all right to let out a real snarl when Friday came out from among the flowers.

She was wearing a petunia on one of her long, silky ears. What with being knocked down in the gutter outside and then being rolled in the garden you couldn't see much of her silky coat for the mud. But she knew her manners and how to

make friends with the grownups. She trotted right up to Mrs. Nelson, stood on her hind legs, and laid her paws on Mrs. Nelson's clean white apron. She looked into Mrs. Nelson's face with what would have been a friendly grin if it could have shown through her mask of mud.

"You horrid little beast!" shouted Mrs. Nelson, who didn't know that Friday was trying to be friends. "Take your filthy paws off my apron." She closed the umbrella and stood back to take a good swing with it.

Desmond rushed in to protect his friend. But he needn't have. The way Friday flattened to dodge the umbrella showed that she would make a good fighter, once she had enough practice. Mrs. Nelson took another swing, but she only mowed down a few plants.

By now Gus had caught up Friday in his arms and was trying to explain that Mother had sent him, and that it was all an accident, and that they hadn't intended to harm the garden. But all Mrs. Nelson could say was, "Out! Get off my place and take your ugly, rampaging brutes with you, or I'll call the dog warden and have them shut up!"

So they all went out, Desmond keeping a good watch behind him. Women don't usually throw things at dogs, but he had never seen a woman as mad as Mrs. Nelson. Gus set Friday down and was careful to latch the gate behind him, though that was maybe only good manners. Alf joined them. Nobody spoke a word till they were well down the road.

Then Gus said, "Desmond, I'm ashamed of you! And that goes for you too, Alf."

Desmond and Alf drooped their tails and tried to feel sorry

for what they had done. But it wasn't easy. Friday trotted along looking mighty pleased with herself, and still wearing the pink petunia behind one ear.

"Though I don't really think we did much harm," said Gus. And that was true enough. Dogs have small feet and pick their way. They can chase a woodchuck or a rabbit or cat out of the garden and not harm a single plant. For all the snapping and snarling and barking and wrestling, likely they hadn't broken a single flower except for Friday's petunia—or anyway, not many.

Alf saw them all the way to their house, and said, "Des, old man, I don't know when I've had a better fight lately. Let's do it again soon." That was honest praise from an expert.

Desmond's tail began to wave again, until he remembered that he was still in disgrace, and stopped it.

Of course Gus had to go in and tell Mother about it. Mother said, "Shocking!" But she smiled. "It will be weeks before Mrs. Nelson speaks to me again—I hope! Now take Desmond out on the lawn and give him a good brushing. A real good brushing. Friday's long coat will need a bath."

No dog likes to be washed, especially with perfumed soap. It makes you smell like a drugstore. But being brushed is a treat. Gus knew how to make your whole skin tingle with pleasure.

Desmond went out to join him with his tail waving in the air. It had been a grand morning after all.

chapter four

It was one of those days when you woke up knowing that something exciting was about to happen. You felt it in your stomach, or it made your nose tickle, as though you were almost able to scent what was around the corner in that day. Unfortunately, what hasn't yet happened can't leave a trail, so of course you can't really smell it. At least Desmond couldn't.

But he tried. Maybe it was the baking in the kitchen that meant cookies soon, though even cookies weren't important enough to give that wonderful feeling. It might be the red squirrel chattering in the old maple tree, and asking for a good bark-and-hunt. But somehow that didn't taste right either.

There was another thing on Desmond's mind too, yet not for all the cookies and squirrels in Newtown could he recall it. It was something the reporter had said to Gus, and something that he and Gus had agreed to do. But trying to find a home for Friday, and that lovely fight with Alf in Mrs. Nelson's flower bed had put it right out of his mind. And out of Gus's too.

Mother came out on the back porch to shake the duster, and called to Gus. "You'll need your sleeping bag soon. Bring it downstairs and out on the lawn to air."

All of a sudden Desmond got that nice prickley feeling that meant the happening was really starting. Somehow the sleeping bag was the clue!

Newtown mothers knew almost as much about what their boys were thinking as its dogs did—and that was sometimes even before the boys themselves really knew. The mothers visited around to other houses, much the way the dogs did, and there wasn't a mother in town who hadn't found out what was in the air. The dogs were the same; they could guess that *something was up.*

It was the yearly Expedition! Desmond was almost certain. Girls and boys went on ordinary picnics to the Island. They could go at any time when the weather was good. But the Expedition was much more important. It was wholly a boy-and-dog affair. It happened just once a year and had happened every year since the days of the first white settlers. Some claimed that it might even go back before that, to the Indian days.

Gus came trudging out with the sleeping bag and spread it

in the sunlight to air on the lawn. Desmond got up to sniff at it. The sleeping bag was new and didn't smell of anything except a store. It was a small sleeping bag, just about large enough for Gus himself. Still, Desmond could sleep on top of it once Gus was inside, though this time he would have to share with Friday, as he had been sharing his sleeping mat beside Gus's bed.

The Expedition was never set for any special day. And that was part of the excitement. The only thing was, it had to begin in the evening, when dark had almost come. There had to be bright starlight, or the moon had to be rising. Desmond wondered how the boys managed for that. Then too it had to occur after several hot days, so that the Council Rock on the Island, as smooth and not much wider than a living-room floor, would be warm to sleep on.

Midsummer had plenty of nights that suited. But which one was it going to be? That was what all the secrecy was about, one gang of boys and dogs trying to fool the other gang. If your gang chose the wrong day to go to the Island, and the enemy gang never turned up, you just looked silly and the other gang laughed at you next day. Of course you tried to trick them into making the same mistake.

What had to happen—and somehow it always did—was that both gangs hit on the same evening. Neither side dared start till dusk because the other side might see them and fool them by turning back. But once both gangs started, the one that reached the Island first had won the Council Rock until next year.

It was like two dogs walking round each other, bristling, each trying to guess if the other was going to fight. It was grand!

Gus knew all this, just as well as Desmond. He said, "Come on, you lazy old dog, you! We've got to do some real genuine detecting to discover what night it's going to be. We'll take Friday along too. If she is going to live in Newtown she'd better learn Newtown ways."

Desmond led the way, proudly waving his beautiful tail with its white tip in the air. Next came Gus, trying to look innocent so that no one would suspect that he and Desmond were detecting. Friday came last, and if you like small fluffy dogs—Desmond did, at times—she was really mighty pretty, with her silky, thick coat, her head in the air, and her bouncy trot.

Desmond headed straight for Bill the boxer. Bill didn't move much, except to follow the shade around his private doghouse. He was so rich that he had a fresh bone every day and maybe that kept him busy at home. But somehow all the news in town came to his ears, and he was the center of dog town-gossip.

Gus went up to the big house to talk to Bill's two boys. Desmond and Friday stopped in front of Bill, who was stretched out, pretending as usual that he was asleep.

Desmond winked at Friday, picked up one of Bill's bones, and made loud, crunching noises with it.

"Desmond and that stray puli again!" Bill growled.

Desmond had never heard a dog called a puli before. It

sounded insulting, like pooch or mutt. Bill was certainly in a bad mood today. But Friday didn't seem to mind. She even grinned.

The breeze brought them a smell of fresh paint from behind the house, where Bill's boys kept their small boat. Like a good detective Desmond connected the two clues. Bill's boys were making ready for the Expedition, and of course Bill would have to go along to take care of them. That was what was making Bill so cross. He liked to stay at home.

To make sure that he had guessed right, Desmond asked, "You don't like boats, do you Bill?"

"Boats?" Bill rumbled deep in his throat. "Who said anything about boats? Don't bother me with foolish questions. Run away now and play some idiot game with little What's-her-name. Try chasing airplanes, or biting lumps out of the moon." He got up and shook himself and stalked around to the other side of his house.

Bill was so cross that he had given away another clue. Dogs sometimes said, "Oh, go chase an airplane!" but Bill had said, "Go bite a lump out of the moon!" That was new, and must mean that Bill's thoughts were on the moon because there had to be one for the Expedition.

Gus came out of the house. Desmond and Friday joined him. Gus said, "They're all fixed to go. But of course they won't tell me when, because we're the enemy, the Land Indians. They have to be the Canoe Indians because of their boat."

That was what Bill had been trying to hide from Desmond.

That morning Desmond took his party around to call on

almost every boy and dog in town. But either the boys were of the Canoe Indian tribe and wouldn't give away their plans, or they were Land Indians, like Gus, and wanted to know, as much as he did, when the Expedition would start.

They ran into Gloria herding her charges on their usual walk. Gus didn't stop, because Gloria's young ones were all too small for the Expedition, but Desmond paused for a chat. Of course Gloria didn't belong to either tribe, but some of the Canoe Indian dogs might have given her a useful clue.

Gloria only said, "I don't approve of this Expedition. I never let my children go near the river unless I have a grownup along to share the responsibility."

They went on to try Chubby, who owned more things than he had time for or knew what to do with. His bicycle with the high handlebars leaned against the porch railing, gathering dust and rust. He owned a BB gun, and a radio, and a sort of boat that you could blow up with a pump. What he needed was a dog to help him get started on adventures. But there was no dog here, and Desmond had to leave the detecting to Gus.

Chubby said, "I guess I won't go on the Expedition. I'm too busy." His way of being busy was much like Bill the boxer's. "But look here, Gus, why don't you borrow my boat? I shan't need it." And he even took them down cellar to show it to them.

Gus squatted and spent quite a time looking at it. He even tried the pump to see if it would work. He weighed one of the paddles in his hand, but set it down again. Desmond shivered. He didn't like boats any more than Bill did, though he was a good swimmer.

Gus said finally, "Thanks a lot, Chubby. Only this would make me one of the Canoe Indians, and I can't change sides. Father was always a Land Indian when he was a boy. In those days the two sides fought each other with wet floor mops."

They had to wait until they had reached home before Gus said, "Floor mops! Why didn't we think of them before, you old dog you! I'll bet you the mop's missing from Mother's broom closet. Let's go look."

Mother had gone in the car to market. Gus opened the broom closet. There were brushes of all kinds, but no mop. Gus hunted around the cellar and looked behind every door. Still no floor mop. Desmond sniffed among the coats in the hall closet and even underneath the beds. Friday helped search; she had a good nose, though she didn't really understand what this was all about, not being Newtown born and bred.

Mothers are awfully good at hiding things, like presents, and boxes of candy which mustn't be eaten all at once. And the mop had one of those handles that come off, so it wouldn't be hard to hide.

Gus sat down and looked at Desmond. Desmond looked at Friday. Friday sat down and looked at Gus. If mops had legs to walk with, then Desmond could have followed the trail. But a mop got carried around by a person so it didn't leave any special scent to follow. What did you do now?

"Know what, Desmond?" Gus was trying to puzzle out a clue. "We'll have to go round the town again and ask the other Land Indians to look in *their* broom closets. Girls can't belong to either tribe, and mothers were once girls, a long time ago. So they're kind of neutral, and they get together and compare

their boys. Maybe a Land Indian has packed some doughnuts without eating them all; maybe a Canoe Indian has put a
lick of paint on his boat."

Just like Bill's boys had done, Desmond remembered.

"So the mothers put two and two together, and hid their
mops so we won't be tempted to take them. The kinds with
metal handles sink, and the old ones, with wooden handles,
float downriver and get lost. Either way's bad."

They were out in the road before Gus had finished his explanation. Desmond was thinking what a smart guy Gus was,
and that some day he would make a good detective—almost
as good as Desmond himself.

Gus said suddenly, "Know what? That Expedition's *tonight!* This very night, I bet you!"

Well, that was what Desmond was thinking too.

chapter five

Desmond couldn't help admiring the way Mother had caught the trick of telling something without having to put it into words. Maybe she had picked it up from him. That afternoon she began to make sandwiches: peanut butter and jelly of course, but tuna fish and other kinds as well, many more than Gus would need for just a picnic. Besides, picnic sandwiches were made in the morning, not in the afternoon.

But nobody said the forbidden and magic word—Expedition! Gus helped himself to three big bottles of Coke from the refrigerator, and Mother didn't even say that she thought one would be plenty. Everyone knows you can get very thirsty in the night, and though dogs drank river water, boys weren't allowed to. Mother had brought home two beautiful big bones, the best Desmond had seen in months, with lots of meat still on them. Just to look at them made his mouth water. Then Gus lugged in his sleeping bag from the lawn, and Mother helped him roll and strap it.

Mother looked at the bulging parcel of food, jammed tight into the bulging airplane bag. "I don't know how you're going to carry all this, Gus. We've left out the cookies too."

Desmond had to agree. All those provisions and the sleeping bag would be too big a load even for the garden wheelbarrow. It would almost fill up the trunk of a car! If Desmond and Friday had been sled dogs and Gus got out the sled and they all pushed and pulled it down across the meadow to the river, they might get it there. But they'd need snow for that and the Expedition never came at the same time as snow.

Gus kicked the sleeping-bag roll and said, "I guess I'd better take a camp blanket." He thought some more, and decided. "There's enough sandwiches for all three of us," and he put the bones back into the refrigerator and cast a longing eye at the cookies. But they would still be good tomorrow. Then he slipped two of the Cokes out of the airplane bag. The bag would close without bulging and was certainly a lot lighter. Desmond gave a regretful glance at the refrigerator, where the bones had gone. But after all Gus had given up his Cokes and cookies.

When the three finally started down toward the river it was already dusk, and getting darker. Not really dark of course, and the stars wouldn't brighten up properly for an hour or so. Desmond could smell the river damp, and they had nearly

reached the crossing stones, when something went *slap* . . .
slap . . . *slap.*

"S-s-sh!" said Gus, pausing with one foot in the air.

The sound came again. *Slap* . . . *slap.* . . . Only two this
time.

"It's a Canoe Indian slapping the water with his paddle,"
Gus whispered. "He's signaling to his tribe. We'll have to
hurry."

They went as quietly as they could. Desmond even tried to
stop the tinkling of his Private Eye badge. The sound came
again, closer this time. When they reached the river bank they
found someone there already. It was Alf. Alf for once had
brought his boy, and the sound was Alf's boy slapping mosquitoes on his neck. Gus began to slap too.

Another boy came along, a stranger. He must have been a
visitor at Lucile's house, for it was Sally the spaniel who was
with him. He wasn't a proper Newtown Land Indian, but he
would help balance the numbers of the tribe. Last Christmas
another boy of the Land Tribe had been given a canoe, so he
had deserted to the Canoe Indians. In Newtown real Land
Indians were getting as scarce as two-tailed cats.

Then, of all people, who should appear but Chubby! He
seemed as surprised to find himself on the Expedition as Gus
and Desmond were to see him there. That raised the tribe to
eight, half of them dogs, which made a pretty good mixture
when you wanted adventure.

Chubby asked, whispering, "What do we do now?" and the
stranger too wanted to know what it was all about.

Gus had to explain. "We seize the Island to keep off the

enemy Canoe Indians. If we get there before the others we can claim the land as our own, by right of discovery."

"Let's go then," said Sally's boy, picking up his bundle. "What's keeping us?"

Alf's boy, who was Newtown born, knew the answer to that. "We can't go yet. If the Canoe Indians found out we had landed, they might turn back, just to make our side look silly. That's why its all been such a secret. We have to be sure they are nearly there, then slip over quietly just ahead of them."

"This ought to help us." Chubby pulled a little telescope out of his pocket and began to search the darkening river. Of course Chubby had everything, but it was smart of him to bring along the telescope tonight. Likely the Canoe Indians didn't own a telescope, so they wouldn't be able to see so well.

Sally's boy wanted to know more about the Expedition, and Gus, between slapping at mosquitoes, whispered to him. "Winning the Island makes a heap of difference. When you have a picnic the Council Rock belongs to your side and you can build a fire there, and can see all up and down the river. If anyone of the other side wants to come he has to ask permission, and you can say 'Permission granted!' Even if he's a bigger boy."

Chubby let out a sqeak of excitement. "Something's drifting down the river. Maybe two or three of them. I can only just see them through the telescope. They're a long way off yet."

It wouldn't do to get to the Island too soon, or the canoes would turn back.

Chubby squeaked again, only it was almost a yell this time.

51

"There's a light, a kind of a reddish gleam, on the Council Rock. . . .Oh, and I can't see the canoes any more."

"They may be there already," said Alf's boy.

Four boys grabbed their loads and jumped off the edge of the bank to the crossing stones. Four dogs leaped from stone to stone to show the way in the dusk. Desmond and Alf made a leap for the same stone at the same moment and Desmond got shoved off. Then he grabbed Alf by the hind leg and it was Alf who fell in. Friday crossed from stone to stone, dry-pawed, and Sally, being a water dog, swam as far as she could.

Desmond and Alf were first to reach the beach and had scarcely shaken the water out of their coats when the boys came up behind them.

"We've got to be specially careful," warned Gus in a whisper. "If we find the empty canoes here we'll know who's on the Rock. Then we'll slip back without their seeing us, and have the laugh on them tomorrow for choosing the wrong night."

He threw himself flat on the ground and began to crawl forward, the way a hunter stalks game in the movies. The other boys did the same. The little beach where the Canoe Indians would land was across the tip of the Island. But crawling is slow, hard work. Desmond and the other dogs held back. They knew how important it was for their side to win.

They reached the edge of the other beach, the boys still lying flat so they wouldn't be seen against the sky line. They looked out across the water, now silvery because of the stars.

There wasn't a canoe in sight. Not one.

Desmond heard the sound first, and nudged Gus with his nose. Maybe it was only the ripple of water. No, there was a click and another click, like paddles touching the side of a canoe. The Canoe Tribe were coming round the end of the Island, so they wouldn't be seen!

The first canoe was really a plastic float, the kind you use in a swimming pool. There was no room in it for a dog. The boy got out, put it on his head, and only ankle deep in water, walked ashore. The second boat was like Chubby's, large enough to hold two boys and a dog. It drew more water and the boys had to get out and wade before they could pull it up on the beach. Their dog, a friend of Desmond's, smelled him at once and came along for a chat. But Gus grabbed him by the collar and scratched him behind the ears. He settled down silently beside Desmond and rolled over for Gus to scratch his stomach. He wasn't a very bright dog and anyway Gus knew that there was more than one way to win over the enemy. This was called diplomacy.

Desmond heard the Canoe Indians whispering, "We're here first! But we'll have to wait for reinforcements." And they all turned to look out over the water. If they hadn't they might have spotted the Land Indians, already in possession and trying hard not to bark or laugh.

Desmond knew what to expect because only this morning he had talked to Bill the boxer, and had put two and two together. What he had expected now came into sight. It was Bill the boxer's boat and Bill's boys. At first they seemed to be rowing the boat, or poling it. It was only a little boat, meant to fit on a car roof, but now against the star-speckled water it looked big and dark. It was still some distance from shore when the boys had to get out. One hauled it with the rope in front and the other shoved from behind.

Bill sat in the middle, looking like a picture of Columbus, but without the hat. Discovering America of course. At this time of summer the whole tribe of Canoe Indians could have walked across the river and not got wet above their middles, but as long as they belonged to the Canoe Tribe they had to arrive by boat.

Bill's boys hauled their boat up till it grounded and couldn't drift away. They left Bill sitting there, stepped ashore, and said, "Well, our side is the first anyway. I hope the other side shows up!"

That was the signal.

The Land Indians jumped to their feet, all eight of them together. Gus and Alf's boy, who knew the rules, shouted, "Welcome to the Island, you Canoe Indians!" And all the dogs barked.

When things had quieted down so they could be heard, Bill the boxer's oldest boy asked, "Have we permission to visit the Council Rock?"

Alf's boy was answering, "Permission granted," when Gus said, "There's someone there already, and they've lighted a fire. We thought it might be you Canoe people. It could be anyone. It might even be the 'bridge people.' How about if we all join forces and go together?"

Everyone saw that when you didn't know how strong the enemy might be, it would make sense. Even with nine boys and almost as many dogs you could still be outnumbered and forced to retreat. Bill's boys told Bill to guard the canoes. He was big, with a deep voice, and ought to be able to scare strangers away. Unless of course he started to think and fell asleep.

The Canoe boys took their bundles, as they didn't want to be cut off from supplies if the enemy made a flanking movement. They all started off.

It wasn't far to Council Rock. The dogs were sent ahead to scout. Boys carrying bundles kept tripping over things in the dark and making noises. They had gone only a few yards when Sally gave a loud snuffle. She smelled smoke—and something else too.

Desmond smelled something cooking. It was hard to believe that anyone would be cooking so late after dinner, but the next moment they could see the glow of a fire, and a dark figure sitting beside it. *Professor Wiggins!*

He was roasting a wienie on a long stick.

"Hi, all of you!" called the Professor, who knew every dog in town. And as Gus and Bill's eldest boy came running up the Rock, he asked, "Have I your permission to camp on Council Rock?" All very proper and as it should be.

Gus gave the proper reply: "Permission granted!" And then asked, "Can we sit around your fire, Professor?"

It isn't easy to make a fire, and a fire is a very nice thing to sit around, particularly when darkness folds in. The glow makes a room around the firelight and keeps the rest of the world outside.

Now that the two tribes were at peace they dumped their packs and bags and settled in a ring on the rock. The fire, burned down to hot embers, was just right to cook on. The Canoe Indians had been able to bring lots of provisions in their boats. They cut green sticks and toasted wienies and marshmallows. Gus tried to toast his sandwiches, but most of their insides fell out into the embers, so he shared the others out fairly between Friday and Desmond.

"Gosh!" said Gus suddenly, "a bear!" and pointed with his Coke bottle.

Everyone stopped eating to look. What they saw when it came out of the darkness wasn't quite so big or scarey as a bear. It was only Bill the boxer, who had got tired of just sitting in the boat, and had had to wade ashore like the rest of them. Likely he figured that Columbus discovering America had had to wade ashore too.

He came over to Desmond, slumped down with a sigh, and growled crossly. "This Expedition is a lot of foolishness. I've tried to tell my boys that every year. But I can't let them come here alone."

It was peaceful and nobody wanted to talk much. Desmond was wondering how the Professor happened to be on the Island. Perhaps the Professor caught the thought, for he said:

"You're wondering what brings me here. Looking for Indian relics. I found another this afternoon, but it's only an arrowhead, and not old enough to prove a theory I've been working on." He sounded disappointed.

He took the stone arrowhead out of the big pack beside him and passed it around. Desmond didn't even sniff at it. He was thinking of those two big bones back in the refrigerator at home. Sandwiches didn't last long, once you had swallowed them. What made him still hungrier was that the Canoe Indians had been able to bring along bones for their dogs, as well as all the other things they had carried. The Land Indian dogs had none.

58

"When the weather's fine," went on the Professor, "I sometimes camp here overnight, so I can get to work early in the morning. No one else is liable to come along then and start thinking I'm digging for treasure. That would ruin the site, archaeologically speaking. But secrecy no longer matters, for I fear that my work is ended. I understand that the Highway Department intends to level the Island and use it for an abutment for the new bridge."

Bridge! That was the word that Desmond had been trying to remember. And now it all came back to him. He and Gus had planned to save the Island from the "bridge people," and they hadn't done a thing. Not a thing! They hadn't even discovered who the "bridge people" were, or what they looked like or smelled like, or where they came from. Maybe it still wasn't too late, because no one could have stolen the Island yet, when here were all these boys and dogs sitting on it.

Desmond soon stopped worrying. It was a beautiful night, with a big moon rising somewhere downriver. The breeze blew away the mosquitoes and the Council Rock was warm as a bed, though a trifle hard. The Canoe Indians unrolled their sleeping bags to sit on. Gus wrapped his blanket around his shoulders till he looked like a sure enough Indian. The Professor brewed himself coffee in a can. There was a lovely scent of pine needles from the three great trees that loomed above the Rock. In fact everything would have been perfect if it hadn't been for the *crunch crunch* of those Canoe Indian dogs working at their dinner bones.

Professor Wiggins set aside his coffee to cool, and began answering questions. "This place exactly fits the description of Peace Island in the Indian legends. It was so sacred that when chiefs made peace here they knew that they could trust each other to keep the pledge."

Crunch . . . crunch . . . went those Canoe dogs!

"Now that's what I've been trying to establish. I've got books and papers and early maps of the region to support my contention."

Crunch . . . crunch . . . lick . . . lick! The Canoe dogs were getting to the rich marrow now. Desmond could endure it no longer. He slipped out of the ring of firelight. Friday went with him.

People always brought bones on picnics, and when you left for home you buried your bone for next time. Only, the next time you had a fresh bone and forgot where you had buried the last one. So there must be dozens and dozens of bones on the Island, some of them old but full of rich flavor. There should be plenty for Friday too.

First Desmond went down to the river for a long drink. All the excitement had made his nose dry and it had to be good and damp to smell something two or three inches underground. Then he went back, and remembered almost exactly where he had buried his last bone, less than a month ago.

He hadn't scratched twice before he touched it. He grabbed it up and shook some of the soil off.

Friday had never been to a picnic, so she dug because she saw Desmond digging. What she found was an odd-looking object. It must once have been a jaw because it had a few teeth left in it. It was so old that it had no smell. Still, it would serve to take back, and Friday could pretend to enjoy it, if only to show those Canoe Indian dogs that they weren't the only ones with bones to gnaw.

Professor Wiggins had brewed some more coffee in his can and offered it around. But he had used a salmon can and nobody else much liked the taste, though he kept on sipping at it. He kept on talking too.

"You're right, Gus, about the Expedition. There were the early Indians who had settled along the river because of the fishing, and another tribe who came down from the north and tried to drive them out. Perhaps the boys of the early white settlers who came here caught onto the idea and called themselves Canoe Indians and Land Indians and fought each other over the Island. It was only thirty years ago that I myself got a bloody nose and cut my knuckles on a Canoe Indian's teeth. But the whole thing goes back and back, far beyond those games. Even beyond the early tribes here. Only I can't *prove* anything." He took another thoughtful sip of his coffee.

Desmond, working busily on his bone, hoped that the Canoe dogs would notice that he had one. But Friday, who didn't seem to know what boys ate, took hers to Gus. Gus told her "No," and asked the Professor another question. So what did Friday do but trot over to Professor Wiggins and drop her find at his feet!

The Professor said a polite "Thank you" to Friday, and to show that he valued the gift slipped the odd-looking jawbone into his pocket.

He went on talking. "It happened long before the first white men settled here, Gus, and even the Indians they found had no memory of where the great battle was. They had only the legend about it." He took another sip of the salmon coffee. "The northern Indians had captured the north bank of the river. Legends don't tell us what river, just 'The River.' The River Indians still held the south bank. There was a small island between them, too rocky to be worth planting, and too small for a village. But each side wanted it, perhaps because of pride, or perhaps as a stepping stone from which to invade the other's country. Well, you can guess what happened."

The Canoe Indians had wriggled into their sleeping bags, and didn't want to bother to guess. Some of the Land Tribe were still awake, because a blanket isn't so comfortable on a bare rock. Friday had curled herself on Gus's feet, and Gus still sat upright. Desmond was determined to go on gnawing, if only to show the others how good his bone was. But it wasn't . . . very.

"One evening as soon as it was dusk the River Indians floated silently down in their canoes. The Land Indians waded quietly across from the shore. When the moon rose they joined in battle, and by its light they fought till dawn. That's why the Expedition usually waits for the full moon.

"In the morning all was silent except for a few groans and moans. Here, where we sit now, were the two chiefs of the tribes. As the sun rose, wounded men dragged themselves to the Rock and lay in a circle around their chiefs. Except for grunts of pain they were silent. The chiefs neither moved nor spoke. Nor, when water was brought to them, did they drink. Their wounds were mortal and they knew that the end was near. They were waiting only for hate and enmity to die in their hearts, so that they could make a lasting peace between the two tribes. And their wounded braves waited with them.

"Through the heat of that day and into the chill of the next night they waited, not stirring. Then in the little light that comes before the dawn and which is a hope rather than a promise, one chief staggered painfully to his feet. He said, 'Let there be peace between our people!' And fell. The other chief moved, but could not rise. He said, though his voice was heard by only a few, 'It is peace!' And he too died.

"We do not know where they were buried. We know only that this island became an Island of Peace."

The Canoe Tribe had long ago zipped up their sleeping bags, and of the Land Tribe only Gus was still sitting up and listening. The Professor got stiffly to his feet, like the chief he had talked about, but only to spread his blankets and lie down again.

Gus wrapped his blanket around him and lay down like the other chief. Desmond and Friday wriggled up close to him, one on each side, to keep him warm.

And peace closed in on the sacred Island.

chapter six

"We'll have to go to our hideout, Desmond," said Gus, "if we want to really think how we are to save the Island."

This was a move that Desmond himself had been considering. For it was curious how getting ready to think always attracted people and dogs to you. Gus and Desmond between the two of them spent so much time in thinking it seemed to bring almost every boy and dog in Newtown around in the course of a morning—and usually just when a nice thought was forming.

Looking back over his shoulder, the way you do when you are trotting away to bury a good bone, Desmond led Gus and Friday to their latest hideout at the bottom of the garden. He hoped that no one noticed where they were going. There had been a time when under-the-porch had been good enough to think in, but dogs and people and mothers had learned to look for them there. So for a time they had changed to the wood-shed. But that got used up too. Then they tried the treehouse, which wasn't so much a hideout as it was hard for visitors to reach. But dogs could scent where they had gone, and their boys would yell, "Hi Gus! Come on down. We know you're up there!"

The new secret thinking-place was the best of all. It looked more like a trash heap than anything else, and no one would imagine living inside such a place, even though it was really a very special kind of brush pile. Last winter an old elm tree at the side of the garden had blown down in a gale. Nobody wanted the wood because elm doesn't burn well, so the sawed-off branches had been piled against the side fence till Father could find someone to take them away, and the lawn would be dry enough so a truck wouldn't leave ruts in it. Then Father was too busy to remember and a grapevine had grown all over the brush pile, making it still more secret.

Desmond had found a way to wiggle inside, right into the heart of the branches. Gus, following with his scout knife, had cut away twigs till there was quite a little room, bigger than Bill's doghouse. It was beautifully hidden, but you still had to be careful, to keep it secret.

Gus went along, whistling to himself as though he weren't going anywhere special. Desmond halted to examine a mole hole, and Friday, who didn't talk but was smart enough, stopped to look up into a tree in case there was a squirrel.

They reached the pile. They all looked around. There was nobody in sight.

"Quick!" said Gus. He squeezed in between the brush pile and the fence, ducked down, and vanished.

Friday and Desmond did the same. That was another good thing. The doorway was at the back and hidden by the fence and the lilac bushes on the further side of it.

Gus scrunched down with his back against the old tree stump, hit his head against a bough, and said, "Ouch!" as usual. Desmond backed in between two other boughs so he could stretch out full length, and Friday lay across Gus's feet, almost as though she owned him.

Gus stopped rubbing the bruise on his head. "We promised ourselves, Desmond, that we would find Friday's people, and save the Island from the 'bridge people.' We didn't find her people, but we did stop that telephone man from stealing her. And we saved her from Mrs. Nelson too. So now we don't need to worry about Friday any more."

Desmond looked at the little brass tag hanging from Friday's collar. Even in the dim light of the hideout it shone bright and new. He could guess what was coming.

"Now Father's got the license for her she isn't a stray any longer. She's ours, and anyone who tries to steal her would go to prison. So she's safe."

Desmond was still puzzled over Friday. Once he had felt sorry for her. Now he liked her a lot. But if she had only lived nearby and not right in his and Gus's house, he would have liked her still more.

"So now we can concentrate on the Island." Gus had ticked off the Friday problem on one finger, and stuck out another to show what he meant. "That ought to make it a lot easier. Of course other people may be able to help. Father has his 'Save the Island' committee, and there's the reporter and Professor Wiggins who don't want to lose it. But the Island is really ours because we captured it from the Canoe Indians. So it's our job to save it."

That made sense, but it was still very puzzling. If Alf stole a bone of yours when you weren't looking, you waited for your chance and stole it back again. Unless of course he had buried it where you couldn't find it. But you couldn't bury an island.

Gus sounded as puzzled as Desmond felt when he said, "It has something to do with votes. People with a lot of votes can take most anything from people who haven't got so many votes. Father says they could even pull down our house if they wanted to make a road through our garden. Why, they could even take this hideout!"

Desmond pricked up his ears. That would be terrible! He glanced at Friday to see what she thought. Her bright little eyes peered out at Desmond through her long bangs, but she yawned. She couldn't see the danger of those votes.

"We've got to do something," Gus repeated. "Only I don't know what. Don't just lie there with your long tongue hanging out. *Think* of something!"

Desmond hauled in his tongue so fast he nearly swallowed it, and shook his head so that his Private Eye badge tinkled.

Being a detective who had worked on several cases with the state trooper, he was surprised that Gus hadn't thought of the one solution.

Gus jumped up. "*I* know. We'll go ask the trooper. Ouch!" He had hit his head on the bough again. The hideout was far too small to get excited in.

They crawled out and went up the garden path, without anyone suspecting what they were about to do. They headed for the drugstore to ask Mr. Mason if the trooper had been in yet for his morning coffee. But they didn't get far, for on the way a car stopped and the trooper himself leaned out to ask, "Going anywhere special, Gus?" He was in his own private car this time, so he could take a passenger. Or even three.

"There's a sight of strangers coming to town soon, on account of this bridge hearing," he told them as they scrambled in. "There's bound to be double parking, and that means traffic snarls for me to iron out. And where there's a crowd there's bound to be a few bad characters looking for what they can pick up. If you'd keep your eyes skinned it would help."

Desmond in the back seat sat up straighter. The trooper was again asking for assistance.

"Or maybe," went on the trooper, "you're already busy on a case?"

Gus said he was—or he wasn't, he didn't exactly know, because he was looking for votes. And he told what he had heard from Professor Wiggins, from the reporter, and from Father about the Island.

When Gus had finished the trooper said, "Your Father's right. They can do most anything with votes. And that's what this hearing is about. If the 'bridge people' have the most votes at the hearing they can take the Island away from Newtown. But if Newtown has more, then they can't touch the Island."

Desmond sank back on the seat. This was disappointing. They had counted on the trooper's explanation but it hadn't been of any real help. Every so often even the smartest dog comes across something that not even his own boy can explain to him. Like, for instance, how so many people can crowd inside the radio box and talk and sing, and never need meals or anything. And this time the puzzle was votes. He had never set eyes on a vote, he didn't know how big it was, what color it was, or what it smelled like. Gus hadn't explained.

They parked opposite the Town Hall, where the hearing was to be. Men who looked like the reporter only with bigger cameras, were going in. Someone hung a big box over the doorway. It shouted: *"Testing . . . testing . . . testing . . . One, two, three, four. That better, George?"* A few Newtown people were talking together, and others, strangers in town, stood in another group across the way. Surely not enough people to steal a big thing like the Island!

The trooper glanced at his watch and said, "Things won't warm up here for a while yet. I'll go check in at the barracks." And he drove off.

"What we need badly," said Gus desperately, "is lots of people with votes—lots of votes."

Only, how to find them if you weren't at all sure what they were? "I'll just have to go round," said Gus, "and ask everyone we know. Someone is bound to have some to spare."

It was then that Alf trotted up, all excited by the crowd and the strange cars. Alf went around so much he was almost certain to know about votes. Desmond asked him.

"Votes?" said Alf briskly. "Oh, you mean *goats*." Alf seldom stopped to listen and never stopped to think. "You want some, Des old man? There's three or four on the farm north of the town. I'll go see if I can borrow some for you." And he raced off down the street, lickety cut. No use barking after him either.

Gus frowned so hard that Desmond knew he was thinking. Gus said, "There are all kinds of rules about who can vote, so it would be useless to ask just anyone to vote against the bridge, because maybe they wouldn't be allowed to. We'd best ask Professor Wiggins first, because he reads so much he knows everything and is easy to understand. We could have asked the Book Boy just as well, only he's away at summer camp."

Desmond started back down the street, Gus and Friday following. Only as it turned out it wasn't the Book Boy who was away, but his father, the Professor.

Duchess the dachshund met them at the door. And there in the kitchen was the Book Boy, eating cornflakes and milk, with a book propped against the milk jug as he read. He talked as he ate and he ate as he read. He sounded as though he were reading aloud, not just talking, when he spoke to Gus.

"The answer to your inquiry, Gus, is that for all practical purposes Pop may be assumed to be temporarily nonexistent." And he poured more milk on his cereal.

"You mean he's not here?" asked Gus.

"That," said the Book Boy, "is the nub of the matter. He sent a wire to me, saying 'Hold the fort' which I construed to mean 'Come and look after the house.' So Duchess and I hitchhiked home, because Pop had forgotten to send money for the fare. We arrived in good time, for he was waving a bone in one hand, locking the door with the other, and trying to give the keys to a puzzled taxi driver."

Gus seemed to understand, for he asked, "Where did he go?"

"That is a matter for surmise. He told the taxi driver 'Airport,' but doubtless he had a more remote destination."

Then the telephone rang, and the Book Boy said, "Kindly answer that Gus. If need be, tell the caller that I am immersed in the study of electronics and must not be disturbed."

Gus said into the phone, "This is Gus . . . no, he's probably at a remote destination somewhere . . . I wouldn't know which one, and as for bones, he's got shelves and shelves of them right here. Why don't you ask the Newtown *Gazette?* They know everything."

"That's all the information I could afford them," said the Book Boy as Gus hung up. "But they keep on calling. You would think that Pop had robbed a bank." He helped himself to more cereal and turned over a page. "I have to sit here and answer every call, because it might be Pop asking for some papers or for his pyjamas. There are times when I feel he is somewhat remote from the realities of life."

Desmond had stopped listening. There were so many words that he didn't understand, and he had been enjoying the lovely smells that drifted in from the back porch. He went to the screen door and nosed it open a crack. Duchess pushed it right open and the three dogs went out to the porch. There on the floor were two plates piled high with lamb chops and eggs and bacon.

"Help yourself," invited the Duchess. "You'll be doing me a favor. You saw my boy spooning up cornflakes and milk. That's all he ever eats when his father is away. Eating chops means using a fork and knife, and that means taking his eyes off his book. Mrs. Jones comes in every day to clean up, and as soon as she has cooked another meal he sets it out here for me, and I have to eat it for him."

"No harm to that," remarked Desmond, between mouthfuls. "You're not a dachshund or you wouldn't say that! I have to watch my figure."

Yes indeed. Dachshunds are low-slung, because of their short legs, and their undersides nearly rub the ground anyway. "What you need," said Desmond, "is another dog. Two stomachs are better than one." He glanced sideways at Friday, who was tucking into the other plate of food most valiantly.

"And two heads would be better than one, for looking after my boy and his father," agreed the Duchess. "They neither of them have sense enough to come in out of the rain. If I could herd them together, the way Gloria does with her little ones, I might be able to handle the problem. But first one goes away, and then the other. It's extremely frustrating."

Desmond looked at Friday and had a bright idea. "What you need is a helper, Duchess. A quiet little puli"—Bill's word slipped out—"who wouldn't interrupt their reading, but would lie down on their feet and keep them from wandering off."

"I don't know any pulis around Newtown, but that's quite a notion of yours." Duchess looked at Friday, and seemed to like what she saw. "I don't know why it has to be a puli, though."

The screen door opened and Gus and the Book Boy came out. The Book Boy picked up the emptied plates. He patted Duchess and said, "You really are a help. I don't know what I'd do without you."

"The Book Boy doesn't seem to know if his father will be back in time to vote at the hearing," said Gus, when they were outside in the street again. "What's more he doesn't know where his father is. He says voting's much harder than you'd think, from marking a special paper to pulling the right levers inside a box, and if you don't do it exactly right it doesn't count. It's not just holding up your hand, like in school. But now we've really got to hurry, because more cars and people are coming into town every minute. And I bet they're all going to the hearing."

Gus had had his try. The Book Boy was certainly the brainiest of all the Newtown boys, but Bill the boxer was the brainiest of all the Newtown dogs. It was Desmond's turn now, so he led the other two straight to where Bill lived.

"We'll go ask Bill's boys if they know someone who has a vote," said Gus, not quite getting Desmond's plan. He ran up the porch steps, called, "Anybody home?" and went right in.

Bill was awake. Desmond told him what the Book Boy had said about the vote being a piece of paper or a lever inside a box or holding up your hand as in school. Of course a vote couldn't be all those things which didn't look alike or smell alike.

Bill gave a scornful snort. "That Book Boy's crazy, and I always said so! You don't learn anything out of books— anything important, that is. I'm glad you and your little Hungarian friend have come to ask me. I can give it to you straight. It's no use your boy asking my boys for a vote, because they haven't any. Even Chubby doesn't own one. A vote is something dangerous, like a car or a rifle, and no boy's given one till he's grown up."

Desmond almost forgot to listen. He was staring at Friday. "You mean Friday's a Hungarian?" he asked.

"Of course. Hungarian sheep dog, a puli. They're rare, but you meet them at dog shows now and then. Didn't you know?"

Bill had scarcely said it when Gus came running out again. He said, "We've simply *got* to hurry, Desmond! All the votes are down at the hearing and nobody's allowed to lend one to someone else."

It was no good telling Gus what he had just learned from Bill: that a boy hadn't the right to a vote. And that a vote was something like a car or a rifle, which meant that it would smell of iron and oil. But as they got closer to the Town Hall he realized how difficult it was going to be to follow any scent here. Cars were parked all around the parking lot, reaching right out into Main Street. And all the cars smelled of iron and were oily. Some had strange dogs in them, and a strange boy or two. Still more cars were driving up, or cruising around, looking for places to park. Men and women were going into the Town Hall.

Desmond sniffed at everything he could. Friday did the same. Sally the spaniel happened along and Desmond told her what they were trying to find. Then two others came along and pretty soon most of the Newtown dogs were sniffing around cars and people, trying to track down votes—except Alf, who had gone off, and Bill, who hadn't stirred from his own doghouse. The boys had gathered outside the hall door to listen to what the loudspeaker was saying.

It was all pretty exciting.

chapter seven

Now you can't have a bunch of Newtown dogs going up and down the street, sniffing at cars and strangers, without the stranger's dogs in the parked cars going almost crazy to know what all the sniffing is about. The dogs in the cars started to bark and yap and ask what was going on. But the Newtown dogs weren't telling. If they found any votes, they didn't intend to share them with out-of-towners.

Some of the men and women who had come late for the meeting wouldn't stop to be sniffed at, and batted at the Newtown dogs with bags and newspapers. That began to seem like a fine game, with the dogs rushing in to play with the strangers.

76

And all the time the voices coming out of the meeting from the box over the doorway got more and more excited and angry. When dogs hear their owners getting all riled up, they get riled up too. The dogs inside the cars were barking and jumping from seat to seat, and sticking their noses out of the half-closed windows and yelling just what they would do to the Newtown dogs, if only they could get at them.

And all the time things got more and more stirred up. Out-of-town boys, who jumped out of their cars, joined the Newtown boys to listen to the loudspeaker. Someone inside was using strange words, like "obstructive yokels" and others were shouting back "greedy profiteers!" and someone was making a banging noise and bellowing "Order! Order!" The words were new to Desmond, but the voices sounded hopping mad. He was glad to be safely outside. People might start using their votes, and if votes were like cars and rifles, they might be dangerous if not properly handled.

A big out-of-town dog, maybe part Alsatian, jumped out of an open car and made suddenly for Friday. Desmond saw his duty and raced to stop the assault. But there was no need. Bertram the bulldog had waddled up on his bow legs, opened his jaw and closed it over half the head of the Alsatian, and kept on smiling. Bertram's ancestors had been bred for fighting and he was too professional to get annoyed.

Another stranger ran to help the Alsatian. Then another dog squeezed out through a part-opened car window. Desmond and Sally and Friday tried to help Bertram, who couldn't really fight with his mouth full.

An out-of-town boy yelled, "That's not fair! Three against

77

two!" He opened his car door and told his dog, "Go get 'em, Tige!"

Tige was built like Alf, only bigger. Sally had smooth, rounded teeth, like all spaniels, and Friday had never learned to fight. Desmond found himself facing three strange dogs at

once. He used an old trick of Alf's—a quick nip, and off
again, then back for another quick grab. Twice he got rolled
over and Tige had him by a hind leg. Then another Newtown
dog came to help.

Out-of-town boys ran one after another down the rows of

parked cars, opening the doors to let out their frantic dogs. Some of the dogs didn't even know each other, so right away they started a few private contests. There were two-dog wrestlings, there were three-, and pretty soon there were four-dog wrestlings, as well as a few free-for-alls, with anyone who happened to be close at hand, Newtown dog or stranger.

You never heard such barks and snaps and yowls in all your life. Oh, it was grand!

Desmond saw Sally latch onto the tail of her enemy. He yelped with dismay and tore off down the road. Sally still hung on. Friday stood on her hind legs and used her hard little paws like a boxer or a cat. The blows were good strong ones too. It was a new method, that no one had seen before, and certainly the dog she was fighting hadn't. Maybe he thought she would peck or sting as well. He lit out to join the kind of fight he understood.

Desmond was in one of those scrimmages where you grabbed one dog, another dog grabbed you, and you ended up in a fight with two more—or on your back. Just everybody got into the fun, Newtowners, out-of-towners, and even a yapping peke and a lumbering St. Bernard. Boys who had let their dogs out of cars whistled and called. It all added to the noise and joyous confusion.

Then down the road cantered Alf and three goats. Alf barked, "Got your goats, Des, old boy. How d'you want to use 'em?"

He slowed to a trot. The goats didn't. They put on speed, lowered their horns, and charged. Alf had to tuck in his tail and break into a gallop. He dodged around a group of dogs whose boys were trying to separate them. The goats charged straight through, and knocked over two dogs and a boy who had bent over to fasten a leash.

Desmond had to stop fighting to laugh. Wherever Alf went those goats charged after him. Whenever he dodged, those goats cut corners, or lowered their heads and went slap through. Dogs let go of each other and made for their home cars.

Gus still stood at the doorway, listening to the hearing. Desmond heard him whistle, and a dog should answer when called. It's a rule. He and Friday trotted over.

"I'm ashamed of you both," said Gus sternly. "And specially of you, Desmond. . . ."

He was brushed aside by people pouring, like angry bees from a hive, out of the doorway. The reporter was one of the first. He had to be first when something exciting happened. He caught sight of Alf and the goats, who were still driving surprised dogs down the street like water washing leaves down a gutter.

The reporter, with his camera up to his eyes, raced after them shouting, "Hold it! Hold it!" Twice a goat nearly got him, but he jumped aside. He turned back, reloading his camera at the moment Mrs. Nelson burst out of the Town Hall. And was she mad!

"I've never been so insulted in all my life!" she scolded. She had hold of the arm of a man she called Mr. Chairman. "You let them shout me down and spoil my whole speech!" She shook his arm. "And then you adjourned the meeting without taking a vote. The Bridge side would have won of course!"

The reporter came hurrying up with his camera and a little tape recorder. Desmond recognized it because he had once given an interview into it. Now he raised his head to show his beautiful white-shirt front, and his badge, ready to be interviewed again. But the reporter held the mike out to Mr. Chairman and asked:

"May I have your version of the meeting, sir?" He put the microphone into the man's hand and held the camera up, ready to click.

Mr. Chairman said, "I heard a dog fight going on outside, and boys shouting. We all did. The Hall began to empty when. . . ."

Mrs. Nelson caught sight of Friday. "I know who started the dog fight! I know who's to blame for stopping the meeting. Just as you were when you ruined my garden. You cur. Take that!" She swung her handbag at Friday.

It was so quick that Friday had no time to run. But she suddenly dropped flat as a rug and the heavy handbag barely brushed her fur. Mrs. Nelson's handbag swung around, tangled for an instant with the cord of the microphone, and finished with a hearty bang on Mr. Chairman's left ear!

The reporter's camera went on clicking.

By now the "stranger dogs" had been driven off in their cars. The Newtown boys were sorting out their own dogs. Alf had trotted off down the road, his goats bleating behind him. All the nice excitement was over. When the trooper drove up to talk to the reporter and Mr. Chairman they hadn't a lot to tell him. Desmond had done his job and kept an eye on things as he had promised to do, though nobody seemed to realize that. The votes that everyone had wanted so badly hadn't been needed after all. Next week it seemed there was to be another hearing.

So far as Desmond was concerned Newtown couldn't have too many such wonderful hearings!

chapter eight

Here they were again, all three of them, Gus, Desmond, and Friday, in their brush-pile hideout. Likely enough there was scarcely a boy or a dog to be seen on any street in Newtown. Some would be down by the river, others in their cellar rumpus room or up in their bedrooms, waiting till trouble had blown over. All because of what had happened at the hearing.

Desmond had been through it all before, and knew that Gus was right to be cautious. You never knew what people would think.

Grownups never seemed to understand that whenever something interesting happened dogs and boys just had to go and watch. If something exciting was going on, they just as naturally got mixed up in it. Then what had started out to be no more than a Scout patrol or an ordinary parade turned into one of the nicest, toughest, and most good-natured brawls that anyone could hope for.

The trouble was that people who were dogless, or had grown too old to go around with dogs, became envious, and started to say, "It's those dratted dogs again. Really, something must be done about them!" All over Newtown people would call up on the telephone trying to discover who the ringleaders had been. Of course there were no ringleaders. Everyone had joined in who wanted to, from Alf's goats to Mrs. Nelson. That was what made it such fun.

The telephone rang once more, up in the house, by the open kitchen window, and Desmond could hear it plainly down in the hideout. Desmond grinned at Gus and Gus grinned back. They knew that Mother would answer as usual, "No, I'm sorry, I don't know where Gus can be. . . . Excuse me, I have something on the stove."

Mothers always tell the truth, but they don't tell more than they need to. When Gus had taken the warm doughnuts and a bottle of Coke, Mother must have known they were laying in supplies for a siege, and likely were somewhere within call.

The telephone rang again and again. "It's the enemy blowing trumpets outside our castle walls," said Gus with a chuckle. Somehow that made the hideout seem even more snug.

Now was the time, when everything was peaceful, for Desmond to tell Gus what Bill had said about Friday. A dog can't talk out loud to his boy, but if he thinks hard enough, some of his thoughts get into his boy's head, if it isn't busy with other thoughts.

"Friday . . . Friday . . . Friday," Desmond kept on thinking.

"Friday isn't to blame." Gus began to get Desmond's thought. "All she did was duck when Mrs. Nelson swung her handbag."

"Bill says Friday's a puli, a Hungarian sheep dog. . . . Friday's a Hungarian sheep dog. . . . Pulis are. . . ." Desmond kept on.

"Bill and Miss Petty the peke missed all the fun," said Gus. "But pekes can't fight and Bill won't."

"Puli . . . Friday . . . Hungarian sheep dog . . . Friday." Desmond thought so hard it almost made his teeth ache.

"Listen!" said Gus. Desmond and Friday cocked their ears. "There's a car stopping in front of our house. I think it's the reporter."

Desmond tried once more. "Puli . . . reporter . . . Hungarian . . . reporter . . ." but got so mixed up he had to stop.

The engine stopped and there was a long silence—so long that the reporter could have gulped a cup of Mother's coffee if he had used a lot of cream to cool it. It seemed ages before the starter whirred and the reporter drove off.

A moment later the car was coming back again. It didn't stop this time. It went on to next door and turned in, then stopped, not far from the other side of the fence.

A voice said, "If I lived where Gus does, and wanted a hidey hole where I could sit and think, I couldn't find anything handier than this brush pile. Only I'd need a guide dog, like Desmond, to lead me in."

"It's the reporter," said Gus. "He must have guessed where we are. He'll be able to tell us if it's safe to come out of hiding, because he knows everything that ever happens in Newtown."

Desmond hopped over Friday and was out in a flash. He showed the reporter the best place to climb over the fence and how to crouch down, move aside a small branch as Gus did, and crawl in on his hands and knees. There was just enough room for him, and if he had brought along his camera and tape recorder he would have had to leave them outside. It was dim after the sunshine and of course he bumped his head and said "Ouch!" as Gus always did. He was really a nice guy.

Friday had to lie across Gus's legs to make room. The reporter doubled his knees up to his chin so that Desmond had room to come in, too. Somehow the reporter managed to wiggle a notebook and ballpoint pen out of his pocket.

He rested the notebook on Desmond's back and said, "Give!"

There was nothing to give, as far as Desmond could see, for the doughnuts had somehow vanished, the Coke bottle was empty, and humans, oddly enough, don't get much enjoyment out of a bone. Perhaps the reporter wasn't really hungry. But it appeared he was hungry for news, that being what reporters feed on.

"Start at the beginning, Gus," he said, "when you and the other boys and dogs were listening to the loudspeaker outside the Town Hall. Tell me what started the ruckus."

Gus told, pretty much as Desmond would have told it, about how Desmond had gone gallantly to the aid of Bertram,

who had waddled up to the assistance of Friday. And then
how every dog from the out-of-towners' cars had joined in.

"So it was you that started it all, little lady?" The reporter
scratched Friday behind the ear. "For once Mrs. Nelson was
right." And he gave Desmond a pat to show that he thought
Desmond had been brave to go to Friday's rescue. Humans
were peculiar about lots of things, one of the chief ones being
their feeling about fights. Didn't humans ever get into fights
just for the fun of it?

Gus also told about Alf bringing the goats, but of course
he didn't know that Alf had got mixed up between goats and
votes.

"I guess now we've got all the facts for the paper." The
reporter managed to squeeze the notebook back into his

pocket, though he nearly tucked Desmond's ear in along with it. "*Dog Lost on Island.*" He was talking in headlines. "*Bridge Threatens Island. Dogs and Goats Break Up Bridge Hearing. Prominent Citizen Assaults Chairman.* The trouble is," he added, "they don't seem to tie together. There's something missing."

"The Professor's missing," suggested Gus. "At least he's been gone several days, and nobody knows where he went."

"Professor J. Bartley Wiggins." Out came the notebook again. "There's been three professors, or maybe important doctors, ringing up the *Gazette* and using long scientific words. They seemed to say that Professor Wiggins had shown them a rare jawbone, human it was, and very old. He had told them about it and it seems they can hardly sleep till they know more about it."

Gus looked at Desmond; Desmond looked at Friday. It certainly was a puzzle. Where did that jawbone come into the story?

"The funny thing is," said the reporter, "one of those professors told the others about a fellow named Gus. Seems he had answered the phone at the Professor's house and said, 'Why don't you ask the Newtown *Gazette?* They know everything.' Now that was a mighty nice thing for Gus to say about my paper. But how come those professors had been talking to Gus?"

There wasn't anything Gus could tell, except that he had answered the phone for the Book Boy.

So the reporter started to get up again. He straightened his cramped legs.

"Instead of one story," he said, "I've got four or five little ones that don't hitch together. And a missing scientist on top of that. Maybe I'll want to come share your hideout if my editor gets rough about this."

Gus said he would be welcome, but if he did come to bring a tarpaulin, as it might rain. He said he would, and crawled out of the brush pile.

Now there were only the three of them left in the hideout, if you didn't count a spider or two. They could stretch out and think—if only they knew what to think about.

Gus was the first to get an idea, only it didn't help very much. "You know, Desmond, if we could do something really good, people might forget that we had upset their old Town Meeting."

That was like Gus. It was Friday and Alf and Desmond who had upset the meeting, and not Gus. But Gus always stood by his friends, even when you came from the river bank all wet and muddy and brought an old dead fish into the house.

"But I can't think of anything really good for us to do," he said.

Desmond began to scratch behind his ear. Everyone seemed to want to find Professor Wiggins. Perhaps if they. . . .

"If we could just find the Professor," said Gus. "Only we don't know where to start to look."

Desmond scratched behind the other ear. If you lost something, you went to look for it where you had seen it the last time. The last time they had seen the Professor was on the Island!

"The *Island!*" said Gus, who often got a thought without having to scratch behind his ear. "He can't be on the Island. He went off in a taxi to the airport. Oh, well, we'll look there, just to show you're wrong. It would be something to do anyway."

This wasn't an Expedition; it wasn't even a picnic. So they didn't have to ask Mother for anything. Still you can never be sure what mothers are going to say, so they climbed over the fence and went out the back way, down across the meadow, toward the river.

They were halfway across to the Island—Desmond and Friday swimming where they had to and Gus wading almost up to his shorts—when Gus said, "It's like when we were on the Expedition. Someone's here already. I can hear voices. You don't think it's those awful 'bridge people,' do you?"

If it were, of course Gus could tell them that the Island now belonged to the Land Indians and that they must ask permission. There were fresh footprints all over the little beach, and when they waded ashore and shook themselves—at least Desmond and Friday did—Desmond sniffed at the footprints and thought he recognized one set of them. He wanted to tell Gus, but Gus was looking over the narrow neck of land where the Canoe Indians had tied up.

"There's a big rowboat," he whispered. "It's full of boxes and bundles and sticks that might mean tents. Who could it be?"

Desmond wished that Sally were here, with her wonderful sense of smell. But he was sure that he was right about who owned one of the sets of prints. He gave a little whine and ran back to Gus, then put his nose to the trail again. Friday sniffed at it too and gave a single yip to say, "Yes, it is!"

"All right, you two!" said Gus, in the kind of squeaky voice that meant he was excited and was trying not to show it. "I'm coming."

The trail ran through the bushes and past the three big trees to Council Rock. And there, just as before, and as though he hadn't moved since the night of the Expedition, sat the Professor. Only around him, instead of the Canoe and Land Indians sat five young men, two of them with small beards.

"Good morning Gus. Good morning Desmond and Friday," said the Professor politely. "You have come to join my class? You are a little tardy, but we will ignore that. Be seated please while I recapitulate the essential elements of our exacting profession of archaeology."

Desmond stretched out on the nice warm rock to wait. He had detected the Professor when no one else could. The rest was up to Gus.

"The invitation on the notice board read 'Dig with Professor Wiggins.' For that I am not responsible. I detest the word 'dig' when applied to the delicate process of archaeological research."

Desmond gave a sigh. This was very advanced human grown-up talk. When the Professor chatted with Duchess and her friends he spoke quite good English that anyone could understand.

"The scientific approach," continued the Professor, "is to absorb all available information. You have perused copies of my notes and my map of this Island. Now you must sit down and give your imagination free rein. First you feel that you yourself are taking breathless and painful part in the battle that was fought many hundreds, and perhaps a thousand years ago; then you are yourself one of the two mighty chiefs, seated on the same rock here, the fury of battle slowly dying from your heart. Then and only then will your eyes be opened for our foot-by-foot examination of the Island."

Desmond sighed deeply. But he couldn't help listening; the Professor made that battle seem very real. And he knew about fights himself.

"Then, and only then," went on Professor Wiggins, "will you be able to apply those ancient legends to the present-day Island. Then and only then will your eyes be open to the search we will now conduct."

It was a nice warm rock, and if you closed your eyes and put your head on your paws you could listen to this talk all day. Desmond closed his eyes.

When he opened them again the young men were asking questions. They seemed to have been asking them for some time.

"By Dr. Syme's tests, and those of Dr. Motov," said the Professor, "the jawbone is unquestionably Indian, and by the tests has proved to be many hundreds of years older than any previous Indian remains we have found in the eastern states."

"But just where on the island," asked one of the young men, "did you discover the bone? Surely you can tell us that?"

Desmond raised his head to listen. Bones were things he knew about. In fact he was somewhat of an expert on them.

There was a pause. Then the Professor said, "Here on this rock, where we sit now. In my pocket."

"In your *what?*"

"In my pocket. My left coat pocket, if we must be scientifically exact. I don't know how it came to be there. My reputation as a scientist may be shattered, I know. But I have no right to deny you this information."

Desmond wanted to tell, but he didn't know how. It was Gus who raised his right hand as he did in school and said, "Please sir?"

They all turned to look at him, and the Professor said, "Yes. What is it Gus?"

"You put it there yourself," said Gus. "I saw you."

"I suppose I must have. But. . . ."

"Friday gave it to you, Professor Wiggins. She gave the jawbone to me first, but I didn't want it," Gus explained.

"Friday?" said the Professor.

Friday, hearing her name, got up and trotted over to the Professor, stood up on her hind legs in her funny way, and tried to lick his face.

"If only you could talk! If only you could tell us where you found it!" He scratched behind her ears, as though to help her think.

Friday couldn't tell the Professor, but Desmond could tell Gus, because Friday had dug up the bone close to where Desmond had been digging for *his* bone. And he could show Gus where that was. He stood in front of Gus, gave a half-bark, and ran off a short distance, then looked back again.

Gus understood of course. He got up to follow. So did

Professor Wiggins and his class. Desmond led the way and Friday came too. Desmond began to dig; Friday looked puzzled, then she began to dig too, by the root of the small bush where she had found the jawbone. Desmond went to help her. And from the way all those men were staring you'd have thought that never in their lives had they seen a dog dig up a bone before.

"Cameras and measuring rods first," snapped the Professor in an excited voice. "Then we will brush the surface soil inch by inch and stratify." He wasn't exactly dancing because Professors don't. But he was grinning and teetering from foot to foot.

"We'll camp here tonight. We mustn't leave the place unguarded. Go fetch the tents and the cooking gear."

His class raced off to the loaded rowboat.

"I suppose you three will have to be home for lunch," he said to Gus. "I'll be over tomorrow morning. I'll expect the famous bone and the written report on it in the mail tomorrow. But don't tell anyone as we don't want a lot of sightseers getting in our way and asking a lot of questions."

And he remembered to thank Friday, and Desmond too. It was Desmond who had done the real detecting, of course.

chapter nine

Every day was different from every other day, and you never knew what a new day was going to be like. Gus always got up early to find out. And so did Desmond and Friday. Mother did not think it was right for people to go around with nothing in their stomachs, so she gave them their breakfasts before anyone else.

They sat in the porch swing, Gus in the middle and Desmond and Friday on either side, waiting and licking their lips to get the last taste of breakfast, and sniffing the morning air to guess what the weather would be like. At least Desmond was.

"It's Saturday," said Gus, "and you know what that means."

Desmond did. Someone would throw the Newtown *Gazette* on the lawn, and he would pick it up and carry it in to Father. That was what they were waiting for.

"We didn't mean to stop that old hearing. It just happened," Gus pointed out. "But when people read the paper they may think it's all our fault."

It wasn't what you did that mattered, but what people *thought* you did. Every dog knew that, and most boys learned it in time. Grownups had such funny ideas.

Down the street on his bicycle came Frank, the Doctor's youngest son, throwing rolled-up newspapers onto people's front lawns. Mostly they landed in the flowerbeds.

Desmond was out of the swing and down the porch steps before Gus had time to say "Go fetch it!" He picked up the paper from under a rosebush, being especially careful not to slobber on it or leave toothmarks, and raced back. Gus opened the screen door for him just in time.

Father was reading a letter with one hand and putting sugar in his coffee with the other, but he laid down the letter and took the *Gazette*. He said, "Thank you, Desmond!" as usual, spread open the pages, and began to read.

Desmond waited for his reward, usually a piece of hot toast with butter on it.

"Just listen to this," said Father. " 'Early this week our peaceful town was the scene of a furious struggle. A violent altercation developed in the Town Hall at a hearing between those who sought to destroy our Island in the name of Progress, and those who hoped to preserve it for our use and enjoyment. Apparently the angry voices inflamed those who waited outside, and Main Street became the scene of unprecedented strife and confusion.' "

"Well, well!" said Mother, tending the toaster.

"And here's a gem. 'The Chairman of the hearing had barely adjourned the unruly meeting and emerged from the Town Hall before he was insulted and assaulted by a prominent lady of our community.' "

"This I've got to see," said Mother, and went around to read over Father's shoulder.

Desmond waited. He was too proud to beg for his piece of buttered toast or roll, and it seemed as though Father had forgotten. Mother was pointing to bits in the *Gazette*. Father had to point with his nose. And each time they made odd choking sounds, as though they were trying not to laugh. But they couldn't be laughing, because nobody ever laughed over a morning paper. Maybe Gus, who was listening outside, would understand what was happening. Desmond pushed open the screen door and went to join him.

The door slammed behind him, but all Mother said was, "Your coffee's getting cold."

"Of course they will call another hearing," said Father, "and we may not be so lucky again. We can't stage a dog fight like that every time."

Mother asked, "Won't you be late for the office?"

Father said, "I'll try to get hold of Wiggins again, but his phone seems to be busy all the time." Then he came out, waved a hand at Gus, and hurried off up the street.

Desmond jumped from the swing and stood staring at Gus,

asking him as well as he could without words, What do you make of it? Gus said, "You can't really tell, yet."

Mother was smiling as she came out, and her nose wrinkled up as it did when she was pleased about something. She said, "You ruffians may like to see your pictures in the *Gazette*. You're . . . oh, there's the telephone!" and rushed back indoors.

Gus spread the *Gazette* on the porch floor, and lay down on his stomach, that being the best way to read a paper. Desmond and Friday lay down beside him to help.

There was a lovely picture of Friday, the one the reporter had taken of her in his car, and under it were some words that Gus said meant *Mystery Lady of the Island*. There was one of Gus and Desmond, which showed Desmond's white-shirt front and his Private-Eye badge. Desmond liked it, because it said *Our Noted Detectives*. There was one of Alf and his goats called *Timely Reinforcements*. The funniest one was of Mrs. Nelson swatting the chairman with her handbag, which was labeled *"You cur! Take that!"* It looked as though the reporter had got things mixed, because that was what Mrs. Nelson had said to Friday, and Friday wasn't in that picture at all.

Gus read other bits, but they were mostly about how everyone in Newtown loved their Island, even the dogs, who had passed a vigorous resolution to that effect outside in Main Street. But it didn't say whether that was good or bad, whatever a resolution was.

Before there were too many pawmarks on it, Gus folded

the paper and took it back indoors. Desmond and Friday went with him, because at times like this it is best to stick together. Gus gave Desmond his piece of toast from the table, and they all tiptoed out again, because Mother was telephoning.

"Father and Mother aren't a bit upset. But of course they're fond of us, so it doesn't really count," Gus pointed out. "Let's go down to Mr. Mason's and listen to what people are saying."

Of course they met Alf the airedale on the way. He wagged his tail at Gus, and asked, "Wanna nice old boot, Des? The farmer gave it to me for bringing his strayed goats back safely. He slipped it off and threw it to me. . . ."

Threw it *at* you, thought Desmond.

". . . and said, 'Take that, you brute.' So I took it. He was so pleased that he waved his fists at me, and danced around on one leg quite a while. It's up at my place now, if you want it. It's a nice boot, but I can't think what to use it for."

Desmond couldn't either. He wished Alf would go away, because Gus and Desmond and Friday were on their very best behavior, and when Alf was along just anything might happen. So he jogged on a few paces and said, "See you soon, Alf."

"Don't be too sure. There's a kind of conspiracy." Alf looked cautiously around him. "I was just trotting down Main, minding my own business as usual . . . matter of fact I had a date to chase that fat library cat up a tree. . . . But I never got there!"

"Why? What stopped you?" This was interesting. Desmond had never known Alf to be cautious before.

"The Gang nearly got me, Des! All of a sudden everybody seemed to be fond of me, and that's not natural. The supermarket man yelled, 'Well done, Alf!' though mostly he chases me with a broom. That warned me, and when one man and then another tried to pat me I guessed the trick. If you let them, the next thing you know, you're caught by the collar. Keep your eyes skinned, Des old man! Well, so long; and don't take any rubber bones."

It began to happen just in the way Alf had warned it would. A car slowed down and someone pointed and said, "There they are! All three of them. Just like their pictures." But the car drove on, and the danger passed. The minister of the big white church waved to Gus from across the street, and Gus waved back from a safe distance. Twice Desmond had to edge aside when people tried to pat him. Then a woman ran right across the sidewalk, said "Oh, you little darling! How could anyone let you get lost!" and picked up Friday in her arms and hugged her.

Desmond looked at Gus, to ask what he ought to do. Growl, maybe? Gus said, "Good morning, Mrs. Morgenthau!" That was the smartest thing he could have done, for the woman saw right away that she was recognized, and dared not steal Friday the way she had probably intended. She put Friday down.

They had almost reached the drugstore, when Gus said a funny thing. "You know, Desmond, I think people are *pleased* with us because of that piece they read in the paper. I wonder why?"

Desmond couldn't guess. Dogs and boys are always in and out of trouble without knowing why.

"We'll go right in and ask Mr. Mason," Gus said. "Just as we planned."

They were the only customers, except for a voice shut up in the telephone booth. The drugstore cat came out to talk to Desmond, and rubbed against Friday because Friday was Desmond's friend. But that didn't tell much, because cats don't read newspapers.

Mr. Mason was leaning his elbows on the *Gazette* spread out on the counter. He didn't look up until Gus put his money right under his nose. Then he said, "Hi, stranger!" because Gus hadn't been around for quite a while.

He started to pile two scoops of ice cream onto a cone, but Gus said, "Just a single, please Mr. Mason," and pushed his money closer so Mr. Mason could count it.

"That pays for a double today, Gus." Mr. Mason rang up the coins in his cash register. "And I oughtn't to take your money. Know how much I make when people buy Cokes and sandwiches for picnics on the Island? Dollars and dollars, every year. If we had lost the Island at the hearing I'd have been that much out of pocket. You three and Alf and his goats did me a mighty good turn." And he grinned, as most people did when they thought of Alf.

The voice in the telephone booth grew louder because the door had opened. The voice complained, "Jeepers, it's hot in here. There ought to be a fan." It was the reporter.

"You're heating it up, I guess," said Mr. Mason. "Leave the door open."

It's an odd thing, but you just can't help listening to someone talking on the telephone. Gus licked his cone more and

more slowly, and Desmond and Friday stopped watching him
and watched the telephone booth instead.

"Sure I've been to the Professor's home, boss," said the
reporter. "There's nothing there but the boy and his dog. So
back I go to the telephone exchange, and the girl says the

Prof's still on his line; and lets me listen in. And it's him all right, talking about bones and carbon fourteen and strontium tests, whatever they are. . . . What's that, Boss? . . . Sure I'm a reporter, the same as you're an editor. But I can't find what isn't there."

Nobody could. Desmond saw that. And of course the reporter hadn't a good enough nose to discover what wasn't there but had *been* there. He really needed a dog, or a dog and his boy, to help.

"So back I go again, and ask the Prof's boy if I can look around. He don't even take his eyes off his book when he says, 'Help yourself freely. I regret I cannot accompany you, for I must remain here in case the phone rings.' Do I search that house! Boss, there isn't so much as a rat there that talks like the Professor. So back again I go to the exchange, and the Prof's still on the line, only this time talking to a guy named Charles in Washington, and telling him to get a move on.

"What's that? . . . No, he isn't calling from a box, nor from a neighbor's. Sure he might be up a telephone pole, making out he's a lineman, and talking from there. Only he's not."

Desmond wondered if the reporter had made quite sure. Sometimes linemen had little tents like tree houses way up on the poles, and Professor Wiggins might be hiding in one of those. Only he wouldn't be very comfortable, or have anything to eat.

Gus divided the end of his cone with Desmond and Friday. Because it had been a double, he gave them more than usual. Desmond stopped listening to the reporter so he could get the full flavor of his share.

Then in came his friend the trooper. He gave Gus a pat on the shoulder in passing, scratched Desmond behind the ear, and let Friday sniff the nice polish on his leggings. He told Mr. Mason, "Set 'em up for my three friends. I'll take ham and eggs and coffee."

Mr. Mason poured the trooper's coffee, gave Gus three ice-cream cones, and turned to set the bacon cooking when there came a yell from the telephone booth.

"Say, listen, boss! I got an idea. There's someone just come in. . . . I'll call you back."

The trooper set down his cup. "You're going to ask me to find Professor Wiggins," he told the reporter.

"And why not?" asked the reporter.

"Because there's no writ out against him, and he's not listed among Missing Persons. That's why." The trooper poured more cream in his coffee.

Gus put Desmond's and Friday's cones in saucers, and set them on the floor, because dogs can't hold ice-cream cones in their paws the way a boy can. Desmond was just starting on his when the trooper had another notion.

"What you and your *Gazette* need is a good Private Eye."

And they all looked at Desmond!

Desmond swallowed half his cone without really tasting it. He tinkled his badge, and looked at Gus.

"Okay," said Gus. "But it would be cheating, because we know where he is already. Only he asked us not to tell anybody."

"Just tell him to hurry back from wherever he is." The reporter was almost yelling, he was so pleased. "Tell him if he's not back for the next hearing he's liable to lose the Island he's so fond of. Just tell him that."

"I'll hold the reporter here to give you a head start," promised the trooper, "just in case he tries to tail you."

Desmond, Gus, and Friday gulped the last of their ice creams. It was a dreadful shame to have to, but when you're on a case you have to hurry while the scent is still warm.

They were scarcely out in the road before Gus said, "Gosh! It isn't true what I told them. We don't know where Professor Wiggins is. He can't be on the you-know-where as we thought he was, because the reporter says he's telephoning. And there isn't any telephone on the you-know-where!"

Desmond hadn't thought of that. Nor had Friday. They stopped, and looked at Gus.

Why not ask Duchess? thought Desmond. The reporter wouldn't have done that because he couldn't.

Gus got the same idea, only kind of twisted. "Let's ask the Book Boy. Come on, you two! We've got to hurry or the reporter will be on our tails."

So they all trotted on, though Gus dropped to a walk when they met people, so as not to arouse suspicion and have others tag along. When they came to the Professor's house, they looked back. The coast was clear. No one was tailing them.

Gus opened the door, said, "Quick! Before anyone notices us." And they all rushed in.

There was the Book Boy sitting at the same table and maybe reading the same book. This time he wasn't eating cereal, but it wasn't till later that Desmond saw how suspicious that was. There was Duchess the dachshund sitting close beside her boy to keep an eye on him.

"Hi!" said Gus, a little out of breath.

"Should you have come to inquire about Pop," said the Book Boy, without even looking up from what he was reading, "I can afford you no information. None whatsoever. Good-by, and thank you for calling."

Duchess gave Desmond a glance, and led the way into the living room. She was worried, you could see that. "My boy used to study birds and rocks and butterflies, and I could point them out to him when we went for walks. But now it's this electricity, which isn't anything you can see or smell or taste; so it can't be any use to him. What's more he doesn't go for walks any longer. Does your boy ever get like that, Desmond?"

Desmond said it hadn't happened yet, because he took good care of Gus. Duchess said that was all very well, but how could she look after her boy properly when his father needed even more care than he did, and that she was only one dog, not two.

"Another dog would come in handy to help you eat up the leftovers when the Professor is away," Desmond hinted, and licked his lips, because ice cream isn't really filling. "Remember how we helped you clean those dishes last time we were here?"

"There aren't any, any more," said Duchess sharply, "except maybe an old bone or two out in the yard. Help yourself, Desmond. I want to talk to Friday."

That was scarcely polite, but Desmond could overlook it if Duchess managed to persuade Friday to come and live with her. Then Desmond almost gave a yelp of excitement. He guessed what no more leftovers meant. It meant that the Professor was here somewhere, helping to eat them up!

He wandered off toward the back door. Then, when he was out of sight, he cut off up the stairs. The reporter had looked, but not sniffed. Because there were no women in the house, every door was open, and Desmond sniffed everywhere. One room, full of books and papers and things in glass cases, was where the Professor worked. Even a bulldog with a crumpled nose would have known that. The strongest scent was in a bedroom. It was so sharp and clear that the Professor must still be sleeping there, night after night. Maybe last night!

He must tell Gus right away, or show him so that he would understand! Desmond rushed downstairs so fast that when he turned the corner at the bottom his feet slipped on the polished floor, and he bumped into a pair of waders standing beside the front door. And there was the Professor's scent again!

Waders meant water, and water meant the river. If the Professor slept here, but nobody could find him in the daytime, it was because he went out to the Island every day. But wait a minute—Shouldn't the waders be on the Island? No, because the river had been falling lately, so he hadn't needed them this morning and maybe yesterday morning. Now everything was clear, and all that was left was to tell Gus. Or show him.

Gus and the Book Boy were sitting at the kitchen table, Gus saying over and over again, "But you've got to tell where he is. It's important!" And the Book Boy turning over another page, answered, "No comment. Run away. No comment. Don't pester me. No comment." Meaning he wouldn't tell.

Desmond had actually given a soft whine to get Gus's attention when he discovered another clue. It was the Professor's scent again, a good rich one too, right beside the low cupboard on which the telephone sat. The cupboard door was open a crack, so he nosed it open, because maybe the Professor had hidden inside instead of going to the Island today. But there was no room for him because all the space was taken up by what looked like a radio. Two wheels were turning slowly, but silently. It was most disappointing.

Gus gave a squeak of excitement. "It's a tape recorder, like the one the reporter sometimes carries, only bigger." He jumped up from his chair and went to kneel beside Desmond. He put out a hand to twiddle one of the knobs to make the thing talk out loud. . . .

"Don't you dare touch it!" yelled the Book Boy, "and promise you won't tell anyone?"

"Not if you'll tell where your father is."

The Book Boy took off his spectacles and polished them. He seemed amused. "Pop's on the Island, of course, finding more bones and things, and sending them off to be analyzed to find out how old they are."

"He can't be, because he's been telephoning all morning, and there isn't a telephone on the Island," Gus pointed out. "The reporter heard him."

Desmond's tail drooped right down. A minute ago he thought he had solved the whole mystery, and how smart Gus would think he had been to do it all by himself. Now the case was a harder problem than ever. He ought to have remembered what the reporter had told his boss from the drugstore, because a really good detective remembers everything, and puts every clue together.

"Does electronics mean anything to you, Gus?" asked the Book Boy. "No, I guess not. So I'd better explain before you call me a liar."

All Desmond could understand from the explanation was that when the telephone rang the Book Boy answered it. He told it, "This is an answering service. Kindly record your message." Then he set the machine in the cupboard to listen, in just the way the reporter made his smaller machine listen to what you said to it. That let the Book Boy go back to his reading. When Professor Wiggins came home in the evening he listened to the messages in the machine and told it what to answer. Next morning the Book Boy made the machine repeat his father's messages to the telephone, and went back to his reading while it did.

"Here's the way it works," said the Book Boy. He pulled his chair over to the cupboard, fiddled with the black knobs, and said, "This is me, Pop. Just in case I forget to tell you, Gus says you must come back for the next hearing so you can tell how important the Island is because of the old Indians. It was really Desmond who found out about you, but Gus promises not to tell. I guess that's all Pop. Signing off."

He turned a few knobs, and closed the cupboard door. "Pop will listen to that tonight. Easy, once you know some electronics."

Duchess saw them out, because her boy was reading again.

She and Friday looked as though they shared a secret, and Desmond could guess what it was. The best part was when Gus sat right down on the steps, gave Desmond a hug, and said:

"However did you do it? There isn't a smarter dog in all Newtown, or maybe in the whole world, than my old Desmond. It must have been all that ice cream you ate."

chapter ten

"Your paws are twitching. Wake up, Desmond! You're having nightmares."

Gus's voice roused Desmond from a lovely dream, and brought him back to under-the-porch and Gus and Friday. He had been chasing the biggest rabbit anyone could dream of, big as a horse and making a noise almost like an airplane. That meant that in real life something great was going to happen. He grinned rapidly, and gave a squeaky yawn.

"There's nothing for a lazy old dog to grin and yawn about," said Gus. "We've got to watch the people coming in to talk to Father, and make sure Professor Wiggins is with them."

That was why they had crawled in here among the rakes and lawn mower, flower pots and bushel baskets. It wasn't as secret as the brush-pile hideout, but through the latticework in front you could see people coming and going without their seeing you. All the same, Desmond wished that Gus had let him finish the dream. If he had caught that noisy great rabbit it would have been a sure sign that everything was going to turn out all right about the Professor and the Island.

"No sign of the Professor yet," said Gus, "but all six of Father's Save-the-Island committee have gone into his study. So we can go up onto the porch and keep watch from there."

They wriggled out. Gus dusted off his knees, and they all went to sit in the porch swing. They were there only long enough to get it swinging, when Father came out. He told Gus, "You're the very boy we're looking for. There's a rumor going around that you were the last to see our friend Wiggins, and may know where he can be found. Come and tell the committee. We need him badly."

Dogs don't belong on committees. So, as soon as Father and Gus had gone indoors, Desmond and Friday jumped back into the swing. They could hear quite well from there, and still keep an eye out for the Professor.

Someone—Desmond thought it was the bank manager—said to Gus, "Our friend Professor Wiggins went to the airport and disappeared. Did he say anything like 'New York' or 'Chicago' when he last spoke to you?"

"Or 'Rome' or 'Tokyo'?" asked another voice. "He could be just anywhere. I happen to know he speaks six languages."

"No," said Gus. "And it was after he went to the airport

113

that I saw him. But it was a secret, and I promised I wouldn't tell where he was. He'll be back here as soon as he can, because I sent him a message."

"Let's get this straight," said the bank manager. "You saw him after he came back from wherever he went. And it was still later that you sent him your message?"

"Ye . . e . . es," said Gus cautiously.

Outside in the swing Desmond raised his head to peer over the porch rails. Someone he thought he recognized was coming down the street.

"You wrote to him, Gus?" asked Father. "Or did you phone him?"

Gus was still being cautious. "No . . . o. At least not exactly. But I mustn't tell, really I mustn't, because it was a secret."

Desmond wondered how much longer Gus could keep on answering questions, and not break his promises to the Professor and the Book Boy. But he was only half listening, because his eyes were on the road. He was nearly sure . . . and now the man turned in and started up the path. . . .

Professor Wiggins, the person everybody was looking for!

Desmond jumped down from the swing so quickly that he threw Friday out too. Both of them raced down the path. Desmond gave the Professor a soft whine of warning, because Gus was inside the house and could not tell him what was happening.

The Professor understood at once. He said, "My boy told me the committee was meeting here. I'll join them later. But first I want to use the telephone, because mine is so busy."

They all went into the kitchen, as quietly as cats. The Professor even closed the kitchen door behind them. The kitchen phone rang and went on ringing. Desmond could hear it ring in the study too, but no one answered it.

Gus came racing in from the study. "Father says I'm to take all calls, so's not to disturb the committee," he told Professor Wiggins. "But maybe you'll do it for me? You're better at it. Oh, and I'm so glad you've come."

"Thanks for keeping my secret, Gus," said the Professor. "And one good turn deserves another. I'll take the call."

He picked up the phone. "Yes, you have the right number. . . . A Hungarian sheep dog, you say? I've seen pulis in their own country, herding sheep. But not over here. Still I should have guessed." He looked at Friday. And what did that dog do but run over to him as though she wanted to listen too.

"You recognized her breed at once from her picture in the *Gazette?* . . . No, no one has claimed her, for which I am grateful, as she has been of considerable assistance in my research. . . . Oh, that's palaeoethnology. . . . No, I'm afraid I can't stop to explain now. Call me later. And would you be so kind as to clear the line? I have an important call to put through. Thank you."

Desmond looked at Gus to see if he had heard. It was what Bill the boxer had said about Friday, and Desmond hadn't been able to tell Gus. Gus asked, "Friday's a *what*, Professor Wiggins?" But they all had to wait while the Professor called another number and said, "Please reverse the charges."

"So our Friday is a puli, a Hungarian sheep dog!" He

pulled a chair over and sat down to wait for his call. Friday lay down on his feet, to make sure that he stayed there.

"No . . . no . . . no!" he told the telephone. "I'll speak to Charles himself. It's important. Tell him it's Wiggins here. About the Island."

Then, as the Professor waited, a funny thing happened. He smiled at Friday and said something that was all clicks and z's. It was no kind of English that Desmond had ever heard. Could it be Hungarian?

Friday jumped to her feet and stood staring at him through her long bangs. He spoke again. She gave a wriggle of delight and her tail waved wildly. Then she jumped up on his lap and began to lick his face. She must have understood what he was saying, though Desmond hadn't caught a word.

The Professor talked to the phone again. "Yes, Charles . . . Wiggins. . . . Oh, I was just trying my Hungarian on a young friend of mine while I waited for you. But let's get down to business. The new discoveries on the Island have been checked by the experts, and their reports will be sent to you direct. There's no question that they are at least as old as the jawbone, and that makes them several hundred years older than any other Indian remains ever found in the eastern states."

Father and the committee must have heard Professor Wiggins's voice, for they all came trooping into the kitchen. The Professor signed to them to be silent. And they were, though if they had been able to cock their ears they would have.

"Exactly, Charles!" The Professor sounded pleased. "You're perfectly right. Such historic sites must be preserved. And the first step in this instance is to prevent the bridge from being built over the Island. . . . You've done that already? Good for you, Charles! Try to get Washington to declare it a National Monument as soon as possible. . . . You'll need a signed statement from the finder of the jawbone?" He gave Friday a pat and a grin. "That may present some difficulties; but I'll bring her along with me when I come. By the way the finder is a 'she' not a 'he' and turns out to be Hungarian."

Desmond had never seen so many people looking so pleased all at the same time. The committee would have wagged their tails, if they had any to wag—just as Desmond was wagging his—because his friend the Professor was going to give them back their Island.

"We'll both be along next week, as soon as I've had time to put my remaining notes in order. . . . What's that, Charles? Did you say 'You'll be here a darn sight sooner than you think?' Well, let it ride. I must get back to my work. See you next week, Charles." Professor Wiggins replaced the phone.

Three of the committee shook the Professor's hand, and two patted his arm. Father asked, "Do you suppose Washington will act in time?" And they all started talking at once.

Desmond had heard all he needed. He could trust his friend the Professor. He ran to join Gus at the open window—any dog would—when he heard the scream of a fire-engine siren.

There was more than a fire engine to see. A procession was heading down across the river meadow, with boys and bicycles and their dogs, and cars hooting their horns, with the state trooper himself leading the way in his official car. And his siren was wailing too.

"There can't be any fire down by the river," said Gus,

"because there's nothing there to burn. It's more like a parade."

Desmond wanted to run and find out what was happening, but the committee stood in his way. It seemed that they would never go. They kept asking so many questions.

At last Professor Wiggins said, "In sum, the Highway Department has already been instructed to reroute their new road. Charles has already taken the necessary legal steps. But now, if you will excuse me, gentlemen, I must hurry home and prepare my full report for Washington. Perhaps," he turned to Father, "you will allow me to take my colleague with me? She may remind me of things that I would otherwise forget."

Friday had been called a puli and a Hungarian sheep dog, and now she was a colleague too. Yes, colleague, not collie. It was no breed that Desmond had ever heard of, but Friday seemed to understand. Anyway, she kept close to the Professor as they all went out onto the porch.

And there, leaping up the porch steps two at a time to meet them, came the trooper.

"Has anybody seen . . . oh, there you are, Professor Wiggins. We've been combing the whole town for you." The trooper grabbed the Professor by the elbow, as though to make quite sure he would not disappear again. "We had our orders only half an hour ago, and the landing zone is the best we could fix in the time. The fire engine's there in case of trouble. So I guess everything's ready for you."

"So that's what Charles meant by 'You'll be here a darn sight sooner than you think.'" The Professor seemed mildly amused. "He had this all planned before I even called. Just wait till I tell him what I think of him!"

The trooper and Desmond leading the way, they all started down to the landing zone, whatever that might be. It seemed to be a ring of cars down by the river, with a cleared space in the middle. Cleared, that is, of all but Alf the airedale and a couple of firemen who were trying to chase him out of it. Of course nobody could catch Alf right out in the open like that, and he was having a lovely time showing off before all those people.

Suddenly Gus shouted, "There's a whirlybird over our Island! It's flying quite low. Look, I think it's coming this way!"

The people around the landing zone must have heard the whirlybird, which was making a roaring sound much like the giant rabbit that Desmond had chased in his dreams. But of course rabbits don't fly, at least around Newtown. The people honked horns and shouted and waved, but it took more than that to scare Alf. The firemen ran back to their big red engine. Alf sat down and scratched, waiting for someone else to come and play with him.

Desmond and Gus and the Professor and Friday were almost at the landing zone—and so was the whirlybird—when a funny thing happened. The whirlybird stopped, like something hung on a string, right over Alf. Then it began to come down, as though someone were slowly letting out the string.

Gus called, "Look out, Alf!"

Alf could not have heard the warning above the whirlybird's roar, but he felt the draft from the thing's spinning wings and looked up. He was used to being chased away with brooms and garden hoses and most anything people could pick up, but

nothing like this had ever dropped down on him from the clear sky before.

He ran! It was no way Desmond had ever seen a dog run before. It was a comical sort of galloping crawl, almost flat on the ground. His head was turned back over his shoulder to see if the whirlybird was going to grab him by the tail. Desmond was still grinning when Alf shot under the nearest car—and stayed there.

The flying thing sat down as softly as a hen on eggs, right in the middle of the cleared circle. The trooper made a way

for Professor Wiggins and Father's committee through the ring of people and cars. A man in uniform stepped out of the whirlybird and asked, "Professor Wiggins? Honored to meet you, sir! Orders from Washington to take you to the airport, where you will find further instructions and a waiting plane."

The wings were still spinning above the machine, though in a tired sort of way. The man in uniform led the party safely to the door of the whirlybird. Father and his committee tried to give the Professor money for the journey in case he had none. But he said that Charles would have to pay for his little joke, and anyway Washington would give him all he needed.

Professor Wiggins told Friday, "If you have no other engagements, I think we should be going," and introduced her to the people in the machine. The door shut behind them.

The trooper made everyone stand back. There was a gale of wind as the whirlybird rose, and a roar that reminded Desmond of the roaring rabbit of his dreams. He hadn't caught the rabbit, but Friday and the Professor had caught the whirlybird, so his dream had come true after all.

All eyes followed the helicopter as it shrunk in size till it was only a silent speck that disappeared behind the Island. A hundred people and dogs, or maybe a thousand or a million—Desmond was never sure what numbers meant—broke the silence with a rustle that sounded like a sigh of hope.

Then car doors slammed, engines started, and there was a rush of people to ask Father's committee what had happened, and had Newtown lost its Island? And why was the Professor taken away under arrest? Or wasn't he?

"It's going to take hours and hours for Father to tell them," said Gus, "because he'll have to start at the very beginning, and tell it over and over again."

Desmond wanted to wait and hear all the nice things that people would say about him for finding the Professor. Then he remembered it had been a secret, and Gus hadn't told even the committee.

So they headed for home, Desmond tinkling his Private Eye badge to keep up his spirits. He led the way to the hideout, because he wanted to think sad thoughts about losing Friday, and Newtown never being likely to know how much he and Gus had done for it. There wasn't a better place for feeling lonely and misunderstood than the hideout.

But they had no more than settled in and stretched out comfortably, as they could now that there were only two of them, when they heard a voice.

It said, "If I wanted a good place to sit and feel lonesome, I guess I'd come straight to this hideout."

"Our reporter!" said Gus, and Desmond gave a welcoming bark.

The reporter remembered the way in, and bumped his head and said, "Ouch!" as usual. He had his talking box with him, which showed he wanted a real interview, not just something he could scribble down in his notebook. Desmond's tail would have gone up, except that the reporter was sitting on it.

"The Professor's going to save our Island. I got all that guff," said the reporter. "Everyone has by now. What the *Gazette* needs is an exclusive on who found the bones for the Professor, and who found the Professor just in time, when nobody else could. Give!" And he started the little machine whirring softly.

Gus told how Desmond had found Friday on the Island, and how Desmond and Friday had found the first jawbone for the Professor at the time of the Expedition. And how, later on, Desmond and Friday had shown the Professor where the bone had come from, so he could set his class to search for more.

Desmond nudged Gus's elbow to remind him that it was Gus too who had helped the Professor. But the reporter knew that already, for he told the machine, "It was our Noted

Newtown Detectives who painstakingly followed clues invisible even to so noted a scientist as Professor J. Bartley Wiggins, and so led him to his important discovery, which will mean so much to all Newtown."

"That about wraps it up," said the reporter. "A small stray dog gets lost and saves our Island. But we still don't know what brought Friday there."

"Friday isn't just a stray," said Gus. And he told about the Professor recognizing her as a puli.

"A puli, eh? I always said the little lady had class." The reporter sounded pleased. "And there's your missing clue!"

Desmond looked puzzled, and so did Gus.

The reporter had to explain. "Pulis are the latest breed of dogs to come to this country. They're so unusual that I never saw one. Nor had the dogsnatcher, probably. He just fancied Friday's looks, and thought he could sell her for maybe thirty bucks."

Desmond saw how that could happen. Once he had suspected Mrs. Morgenthau of trying to steal Friday.

"Maybe someone offered the dogsnatcher fifty instead of thirty if Friday had her pedigree papers, knowing that a puli would be worth five times as much. The dogsnatcher said he'd fetch the papers, but got scared and beat it. You know how Friday makes friends with everybody, and people stop and talk to her? Every time that happened the dogsnatcher thought they recognized her, and got worse scared. If she was so valuable someone would ask awkward questions about her, maybe the cops. He daren't try to sell her any more, and he daren't keep her.

"So what does he do? He very likely drives a long way off from where he stole her. He takes her for a walk down by a river where there aren't any people about, and tries to lose her. But she keeps following him. He's desperate now. He throws her into the river to drown, and beats her back when she tries to crawl out. She sees an island, and swims to it. Our Island. Friday's Island." The reporter clenched his fists. "I'd give a month's pay to meet that dogsnatcher!"

"Now one more question. If I don't ask it, I guess my editor will ask me. How come. you found the Prof just in time, and sent him a message he was wanted, when I couldn't?"

Of course Gus didn't know the important clue of empty plates instead of leftovers, nor the scent of the Professor in his study and bedroom, nor the very difficult problem of the waders. But he did his best. He told how he had been trying to make the Book Boy say where his father was, when Desmond walked straight up to the telephone cupboard, and opened the cupboard door to show the talking machine inside. And how that explained everything—except how Desmond had known.

"Jeepers!" said the reporter. And then, "Ouch!" because the hideout was too small to get excited in, and he had bumped his head again. He said, "I gotta have that in Desmond's own words. Or nobody's going to believe it. And they won't then."

The reporter held the thing-you-speak-into close to Desmond's mouth. Mostly dogs bark or howl or snarl or growl, which is like people shouting, and only allowed outdoors. But, when they want to, they can use a kind of talk between baying and singing and whining. They don't do it often because no human can understand, not even their own boys; and they don't need it with other dogs because they can talk silently together.

Desmond sang and sang. He explained everything. He would have gone on to tell a few comic stories about Alf that the reporter might not have heard, but the reporter said, "I guess that'll do for now. Never give the public more than it can take." And stopped the machine.

When the reporter had gone, there they were, just the two of them, a dog and his boy, alone. Which is how things ought to be!

DATE DUE